HARDWARE RIVER

RIVER STORIES

ALYSON HAGY

POSEIDON PRESS

NEW YORK LONDON TORONTO SYDNEY TOKYO SINGAPORE

POSEIDON PRESS
Simon & Schuster Building
Rockefeller Center
1230 Avenue of the Americas
New York, New York 10020

POSEIDON PRESS is a registered trademark
of Simon & Schuster

POSEIDON PRESS colophon is a trademark
of Simon & Schuster

Designed by Chris Welch
Manufactured in the United States of America

10   9   8   7   6   5   4   3   2   1

Library of Congress Cataloging-in-Publication Data

Hagy, Alyson Carol.
Hardware River stories / Alyson Hagy.
p.   cm.
Contents: Hardware River—Ballad and sadness—the field of lost
shoes—A seeming mermaid—The grief is always fresh—Native
rest—Kettle of hawks.
I. Title.
PS3558.A32346H3   1991
813'.54—dc20   90-47738
CIP

ISBN 0-671-68111-7
"A Seeming Mermaid" previously appeared
in *The North American Review*.

HARDWARE
RIVER

To my folks at The Old Hundred,
and to Al, Melchora, and Mark

CONTENTS

HARDWARE
RIVER

We are sitting at the Crossroads Inn and Teal is telling me what I ought to know about Lute Dross. Fresh out of college, I am on my way to Iron Gate to teach at the old mission school. After a day on the road, I am wound-up and tired. Teal, my mother's half brother, is mourning the heavy net of frost that has fallen on his north orchard. Together, we make an anxious pair.

Lute Dross could never put his finger on what he wanted, *Teal says*, not exactly. Which don't make him so much different than you. You are cousins on your mama's side, you know, though the Claytons haven't had anything to do with the Drosses for a long, long time. Now Lute wasn't all-around special, I'll grant you that. Not particularly sharp or hard-driving. In fact, he was as plain and common as a pine board. But his plainness made him special in a way that most folks don't choose to remember. Like my own sorry pear trees, so small and stubborn I couldn't kill them if I tried.

It all began the spring the James River rode high enough to float whole boxcars from Lynchburg to Richmond and both bridges over the Rockfish were washed out. Lute's father had run his jury-rigged flatbed off the road to Narrows two years earlier, and the boy was living alone, up the mountain. I guess he ate off the insurance money, I don't really know. He could have been splitting some cordwood to sell, and it seems like I must have seen him at the packing sheds once or twice when the winesaps were rolling in. It's hard to say. Until he started seeing Marlet Keefe, Lute was an easy boy to miss.

He was short and wiry with overlarge hands and stiff, spruce-needle hair that tufted out over his ears. There ain't many people in the south valley who'll admit to thinking much of him—he was terrible quiet and had eyes as dull as muddy quartz. But I saw him at the Crossroads plenty of times, before and after he took up with Marlet, and not a night passed by that his leaving didn't draw a sigh from one body or another. Holloway's niece, for instance, used to go about as tight as a fresh cow when Dross was around. And my oldest girl, Mary, often said there was something odd about him, something that cut him out of the herd, and she was only fifteen at the time. Like a piebald, she told me. Or a buckskin pony. He had a queer way of catching your eye.

Now, I've seen homely men get women. I've watched the ugliest chicken farmer west of Louisa waltz off with both Hersh girls at once simply because he could hammer a dulcimer like he was hammering hot blood in their very own veins. But Lute didn't play no instrument. He didn't sing no songs, didn't smile or spread his cash like cards for the choosing. Far as anybody knew, he didn't have a thing except that farm on the river. Turns out—and I wish I'd seen it coming—he also had the blast-heaving heart of a C&O engine. Nobody guessed it at the time.

That spring, anyway, it rained so hard my peach blossoms were beat right off the branches. I lost forty percent of my first crop. Lute wasn't raising much, some alfalfa or timothy maybe, but the water was laying deep in his fields, feeding the river with what topsoil he did have. Now I know the Hardware River ain't much more than a creek, hardly a spit trough compared to the James or the Rivanna. Yet, as Lute himself might have said, even the smallest streams will have their say. There wasn't much he could do, of course; it ain't possible to slow down them mountain-sprung creeks. I suppose he just watched and whittled and chuckled some because the boys at the foot of the mountain, Jake Milliron and Colter Tate, were the ones who were really going to catch it.

Only, the rain wasn't all that gave us trouble. A ghostly fog covered the mountain for nearly two weeks and made it devilish hard to see. By the time it burned off, my peach trees were unbending, Colter's fields had drained, his bull calves had been taken to market, and that strange, pitiful bird had come to stay.

Colter's wife claims to have heard it first. Or maybe it was one of the kids. But I'll bet my copper-headed cane that the bird had been up at Lute's place before then. Nobody thought to ask him. Anyhow, when it took to hollering in Colter's fields, Colter thought he had a bobcat on his hands, so his wife called the warden. Now everybody knows how excitable Colter's wife is. Still, I had to laugh when the warden told me it was nothing but a heron, a big lopey bird crying in the hollows and sounding

strange. The warden guessed that the rain had confused it—
we don't hardly see them this high in the hills—and he said to
leave it be. It would fly off when it was ready.

I remember telling young Lute the same story, describing a
long-legged bird I had never seen just to cultivate a laugh at
Colter's expense. That's when Lute started showing up at the
Crossroads. He'd mix with me a little, spring that tripwire smile
of his in my direction, and I could see the boy knew a lot he
wasn't telling.

Nobody questioned his coming to town. It must have been
lonely on that mountain; grief and bad weather are enough to
shake any man free. So it shouldn't have been a surprise when
he took up with Marlet. Everybody else had. She was maybe
thirty at the time, and I guess she'd flung about every man in
the valley on one night or another. Not for money, mind you.
It was more like stubbornness than greed with that girl. She
didn't want or need a thing—nothing she'd admit to anyway—
and she was happy to prove it. Like a mink in pond water, she
always made sure that nothing stuck to her fine coat. Didn't
surprise me one whit when Lute began driving off with her
after her shift at the Crossroads was over, though I'll always
wonder why Holloway hired her in the first place. He must've
known she'd cause trouble.

The thing you have to understand is that the Keefes have a
history of being good-looking: tall, long-boned, topped with a
thick crest of hair. Good-looking and mean. Marlet's brothers
were all as mean as hoe-split snakes, and not a soul wet an eye
when the last one was shipped off to the prison in Petersburg.
But if folks were honest, they'd admit that Marlet was the real
sack of venom in the family. Probably the best-looking woman
I've ever seen—and the most dangerous. Your mama will tell
you I'm a hog bladder of wind. She thinks I believe in spirits

and Mosby's ghost and that I ain't breathed a true word since she was baptized in Otter Creek and I wasn't. But what your mama fails to realize, even with a choir of good religion in her ears, is that the devil may give rise to his share of badness, but people's hearts are like seeds when they're set out in this valley. All manner of things take root in fine soil, the terrible and the good. Somebody will always bust loose.

Now don't get me wrong. Black-haired Marlet didn't breathe fire or boil children, and if you saw her yourself, you might be a little disappointed. She was a trunk of a woman, but her shoulders were slim, and she moved with the grace of a willow. I've heard stories about her extra sharp teeth and the bristling hackles between her legs, but that's just talk. She had hair as dark as quarry water, and lots of it, loveliest hanks of hair I've ever seen. Her eyes were dark, tending toward strap-leather brown, and there were times they'd hold the light like plugs of smoldering hickory. She smelled special, too, sort of sticky and cool, the way wood root smells after it's been cut and sanded. She had a fondness for scarves—bright-colored, raggedy things for her head and waist—but she didn't break your heart until she touched you.

Country women are mostly like mayflowers, I guess, lovely in the early spring, then gone. Yet Marlet never dropped a petal. She looked finer every year. She wasn't interested in no husband, either. I'm not sure she was interested in men at all, really, though she always had plenty of them around. The attention, the wanting part, even the love—none of it seemed to have much of an effect on her. Reed Bennett was crazy about her, proposed and everything, and when she turned him down, he said he'd been right all along—Marlet Keefe was a cold bitch with a heart of flint. And he wasn't the only one. Smiley Fitz has always claimed that Haskins lost his eye in a fight over that woman. I've heard whole truckloads of men call her a whore and worse, but it never mattered. They couldn't stay away.

Still and all, it was Lute who made the first move. He was here, drinking longnecks and finishing a plate of fried catfish when he asked to see the cook. Now he must have known who the cook was, everybody did, but Mrs. Holloway was so surprised by his request that she called for Marlet just to see what would happen. When Marlet came out, spatula in one hand, her hair bound up in a kerchief the color of a drought-burnt rose, she walked right up to Lute's table and stood there. Mrs. Holloway says he didn't blush or fidget, he just stared at Marlet with his cap pushed back on his head, and asked if he could buy some of that catfish from her, fresh.

Marlet stared back a while, and told him that she didn't sell anything to anybody.

Trade then, he said. I can barter.

Marlet must've thought he was simple, maybe simple and sweet, because she turned the whole thing into a special kind of lesson. Okay mister, she said. I need some hardwood, half a cord. Deliver it, and you'll get plenty of fish.

I'll be there, he said.

Mrs. Holloway thinks now that maybe she should have warned Lute, reminded him about the Keefes. The entire scene raised her high blood pressure. She remembers the way her ears were clanging when Marlet walked back into the kitchen with her large, dark skirt swishing like a cape. But she never said a word, and who can blame her? She couldn't have known what would happen to Lute.

For my money, a warning would have done him no good. Lute Dross was following the streambed that had cut its way through his head just like he followed the Hardware River into town. I know he had a plan. I was with the sheriff when he

searched the old mountain house, and we could tell the boy had
been up to something that made sense to him.

There are some folks who believe that everything would've
been fine if Lute's mother hadn't died when he was so young.
I know the sheriff clings to that view. But people are always
sniffing for answers beyond the body and soul of a man. Losing
his mama and daddy, and living alone on the mountain surely
had an effect on him. I won't deny that. But the blame, if that's
what you want to call it, can only be laid at one doorstep. Lute
Dross knew what he wanted and he went to get it.

He delivered a load of dry oak to Marlet's the very next night.
He'd been smart and had split most of it into stove-sized pieces,
guessing that's how she would like it. Marlet, being smart in
another way, and maybe a touch grateful too, invited Lute into
her kitchen.

Now I've only been to the Keefe place once, right before the
old man died, but I'll never forget that kitchen. It's a big place,
bare-beamed and square with a stove set into the back wall. The
windows are small—Keefe cut them himself—so it was dark
with shadows and loose ash. Marlet had the place fixed up like
no kitchen I've ever seen. Lots of plants and roots were strung
along those beams to dry, kinds my mama never gathered. A
brace of squirrel hung from a nail, and half a dozen doves were
waiting to be cleaned on the cutting board. The one counter
that wasn't covered with pickling jars was stacked high with all
sorts of nonsense: wire cutters, burlap, insulator knobs. I even
recall a few possum bones. It didn't smell like a woman's kitchen
neither, not with all that fresh meat around. There was a touch
of mint in the air—not much, just enough to remind you it was
summer.

But it's the quilt I think of first. The widest quilt I've ever
seen was stretched across the front wall beside the kitchen door.

It looked solid black, but it wasn't, not completely. Made up of a mess of dark swatches—blacks, blues, greens—and patched together with long, loopy stitches, it didn't seem to have any pattern at all, until I got real close. Then the flowers, tiny things yawning and smacking purple and red, bloomed before my eyes like a rainstorm of open mouths. They were stitched up tight and careful like they could take root forever on that cave-dark surface. The old man had told me that his daughter was a living wonder with a needle, and when I think back on it, that quilt, snipped piecemeal from her skirts and scarves, was a sight to behold. Marlet Keefe was a swift, wicked marvel.

And so you can imagine what happened to Lute Dross when he walked into that kitchen. Firelight flickering on the lids of those pickling jars, air as sultry as a smokehouse or the Crossroads when it's hot and folks have danced the devil from their bones. Catfish, all wrapped and ready, sitting out where Lute would see it and know she'd predicted the hour of his visit. Probably some gutted trout on the chopping block, too. The touch of firelight on Lute's chapped face and those fish scales flashing gold and silver like the corners of Marlet's eyes. He never had a chance. And, Lord knows, he never asked for one. She likely had him on the floor.

Of course, nobody knows for sure. Clare's the only one who might have seen it, but Marlet made her sister stay upstairs. At the time, Lute didn't know any more about Clare than the rest of us did. Marlet had told him to have nothing to do with her, not one thing. And in all the time she saw him, Marlet never took him—or anyone—to the part of the house where Clare was kept. Sheltering Clare was akin to protecting some clean memory of Marlet's own girlhood, I guess, a cleanliness that never was.

I'd like to know how Lute Dross felt that night, going back

to his truck, lingering under a moon no larger than a lathe curl. Breathless, I expect. A little proud, maybe, though he wasn't one to dwell on it. You can see how he might have been anxious, too anxious to stay tangled in Marlet's skirts and the shreds of her hot breath. Imagine him raising his hands toward the breast of that black mountain silhouetted against the sky. Imagine what he saw there.

I doubt Marlet felt a thing. Maybe she laughed while she was washing herself afterward, because she'd seen it so many times— a man confusing a rush of blood with revelation. It didn't really matter. What mattered was that she underestimated Lute Dross. And Clare. I don't know if Clare was watching Lute that night, seeing his palms lift out toward the ridge, but she damn well might have been. Nobody was thinking of her.

Marlet must have gotten pregnant sometime in July. The summer was a hot, wet one. Everybody had a hell of a time putting up their hay. I even had to ask Lute for help. He was seeing Marlet regular by then. And he took a lot of ribbing for it, too—Reed Bennett was always mouthing off. So Lute spent most of his time at the Crossroads drinking alone and making a long glass fence with his bottles. Which was fine with him. He didn't need nobody but Marlet.

Marlet didn't tell anybody she was expecting—not the doctor, not Clare, especially not Lute. She was bound and determined to act like it wasn't worth a mention. And that's what places her hard in my mind, as hard as a sharp chunk of coal. Most women would have made a fuss. Wanted to get married. Or asked for money. Some would have tried to lose the baby or had it scraped out. But not Marlet. She just let it grow big and alive in her belly, silent and turning like a roast on a spit.

Lute knew about the baby, anyway, but he didn't let on to Marlet. He was more interested in his plan. And you can see

how that plan must've taken shape in his mind like the swift
raising of a barn. The joints and beams had come together of
their own accord, and he hadn't even broken a sweat. She underestimated him, like I said, and as icy as she wanted to be, she
couldn't control the ups and downs of her own raging blood.
She and Lute took to fighting. *I want to play cards in Scottsville.*
I want the Peery boys to drive me to Palmyra. She made all sorts
of demands and let herself be seen with three or four other men.
Lute fought with her, sure, but damned if he wasn't preparing
for that baby all along. Maybe he smelled it, some sort of sweet-
ness rising from Marlet's skirts. Maybe her flaring temper gave
her away. All I know is that Lute spent much of that fall working
on his farm. He still rode himself half-blank on Marlet's floor,
but it was the mountain and its silver chain of river that were
winding around his heart.

Finally, Marlet was too full of child for Lute to ignore. She
said, yes, there was a baby. Yes, she planned to keep it. And no,
she laughed, she wasn't sure it was his. Lute told her he'd like
to have the baby to raise. I imagine he asked her real gentle, so
just the tiniest corn kernel of warning rolled among his words.
Marlet responded the way you'd think. She told the son of a
bitch that he'd never lay eyes on it. When he didn't argue, I
expect she took his silence as meekness and retreat. In any case,
Lute Dross walked out of that close, smoky kitchen, and Marlet
Keefe saw him only one more time in her life.

From here on in, the whole business gets more tangled than
my wretched spools of fence wire. Still, as I sort it out now, the
key to the lock is little Clare.

Clare was thirteen years old the summer her sister took up
with Lute. My wife says she must have been older, that a girl
so young would never have done what she did, but my wife is
wrong. I checked at the courthouse. She turned thirteen in June,

when the days in this valley are long and calm, broken only by the deep roll of thunder. I never saw her myself, but her school teacher described her as small, hardly any more consequential than a stalk of milkweed. Apparently she didn't have Marlet's black hair, though her eyes were as dark as any Keefe's. The teacher said she was a pale, brown-haired child who was quiet to the point of worry. But you can bet that ain't how Lute saw her, not once she'd turned his head.

I know she was the one who started it, the game between the two of them, I mean. It must have begun early, not long after Lute was first drunk on the liquor of Marlet's body. So it probably caught him off guard: there he is, on the floor with Marlet, the fire breaking the shadows into shards, gazing past the dip of Marlet's belly, when he sees it—a silky spiral of dove-gray ribbon lying on a shelf. He knows it's not Marlet's. She's not the kind to wear ribbons. It must belong to Clare.

The next thing he finds is a bow of hand-tatted lace, the most delicate thing he's ever seen, tied around a door knob. He pockets it before it catches Marlet's eye. He's not sure what it means, but his instincts tell him that it's not a sign of desperation. It's more like a secret exchange.

Anyhow, Lute started collecting Clare's tokens. They were ribbons mostly, some new, others creased and knotted from use. He must have searched the kitchen while he got dressed, and Marlet was back at the sink. It was harmless enough in the beginning. But later, those baubles just about took possession of him. I've seen the way he arranged them in his house—ribbons braided on lamps, the buttons and marbles in clear glass jugs, lace hanging from the curtain rods. At some point he even started wearing the damn things. When we found him the last time, he had a hair bow the color of a grackle's wing wrapped around and around his cursed neck.

And yet, by then, Marlet thought she knew all about Lute Dross, which probably made him laugh because he and Clare were something she'd never dream. And I expect he developed a habit of checking the second-story windows when he came and went, hoping sweet Clare would show herself. Still, it wasn't until things got bad with Marlet that he decided to have a look at little sister.

It was easy enough to do: he hides in a ditch and waits for the school bus to drop her off. Marlet is at the Crossroads so he don't even have to hide his truck. He just sits and whittles, and crushes blossoms of Queen Anne's lace in his hands. He drifts way off in a daydream because by now Lute's ideas are wrapping him like a heavy river mist. When the bus stops, he doesn't recognize her when she steps onto the sandy shoulder across the road. She looks like a boy—leggy, flat-chested, awkward—until she starts to walk, turning away from him so he can see the polished grain of her maplewood hair falling down her back. That slim, unspoiled Keefe, a doe careful amidst the corn. His heart floats right out of his chest, like an oak leaf taken up by a strong unending current.

So imagine how that next night took shape: he arrives after dark with the heavy cry of that heron bird singing inside his head. He has a gift for Marlet, something he's carved with his own block-hard hands, and then he takes her, shoving with a ferociousness that catches her by surprise. While she's rearranging her wide skirts, careful not to show she is pleased, he takes her again with no more sound than the whisper of burnt resin in the stove, and she lies there, gasping and weak, thinking about the child that's swelling between them, sensing that Lute is somehow different, changed, powerful. He don't say much, though he's tender enough when they're through, and she decides that he is, thankfully, the same—sweet and gullible and dispensable—the same as he's always been.

Marlet is relieved when he leaves early. She fills her shining sink and hums a wandering tune while the wet cloth is limp in her hand. Lute fishes a bent copper bracelet from his pocket, a new present from Clare, and then starts his truck, drifting slowly down the driveway. This time, he don't even glance at the black, frost-laced windows of the upper story, because once he stashes his truck, he'll come back to join his Clare.

Which he does. And Marlet don't hear a thing, not a step or a rustle. Lute Dross slips onto the roof from the front porch and moves from window to window, crouching on the cold, supple tin, looking for the girl. Her room ain't hard to find; it's the only one with furniture. And the window is open, free and loose on its stiff, metal runners—just like he knew it would be.

Now here's where everybody chooses to believe the worst, where they say that Lute ruined himself and gave Marlet the right to hurt him so bad. Everybody talks about how he sullied that girl, that sweet hidden girl who was drawn around herself like a periwinkle shell. But they're wrong—my wife, the sheriff, everybody is dead wrong on this one. Lute Dross didn't sully that girl. He hardly touched her. The only thing of value that he took from her, in all those months of visits, was a promise. He wanted a mother for his child.

Everybody's so damn sure the girl was as hollow as a cornstalk and nearly as brittle. But she'd been leading him to her with a straight line of crumbs. If there was any trap in that room, little Clare was the one who baited it. She was young, but she understood how her black-haired sister was binding her life, and she wanted out. Bad.

People say, if that was so, why didn't she run away? I can only guess that her high, dark bedroom was a lot like Lute's mountain, cresting the sky without a name. The girl lived on her own and had her own ideas.

Either way, the fire was laid.

So Lute keeps visiting Clare in her room at night, whispering to her about how things are going to be for them, while the baby swells in Marlet's belly and she laughs about how she chased Lute Dross right back into the hills. The little boy was born the next spring on the floor of that terrible kitchen with Clare helping out. It's said that Marlet cut the birth cord herself and that childbearing took nothing out of her. If anything, she became more fierce than ever.

Lute came after the boy, of course—just after Easter, not long after I got my potatoes planted. And what transpired then was plain treacherous, there's no other word for it. Every life involved was no more sturdy than a cliff bank.

He arrived in the late afternoon, while the windowpanes were still hot and golden with sun. He even knocked on the door, like he was dropping by to be social. My guess is that Clare was watching from somewhere—through a keyhole or a crack in the floor. For all I know she might have felt the whole thing happen in the soles of her feet. In any case, Marlet opened the door for Lute because she was surprised and amused to see him and, like every other Keefe who ever spit, she was not about to pass on a chance to grin in somebody's face. He went straight for the barrel-stave cradle in the corner, not saying a word, though he was smiling so big that Marlet probably felt like she heard him speak. She told the sheriff later that she'd said her piece months ago; it was her house, her baby. She just picked up that ash-powdered poker and swung.

The blow stopped him in the short run. She hadn't hit him low enough to kill him, but no doubt his head went bright inside, and he folded up next to the wall, right below that nightmare of a quilt. He was out for a few minutes, not long according to the doctor, and when he came around, he was wobbly but sure of himself. I wouldn't blame Marlet for a second if she'd led him out to his truck or called the sheriff. But she did neither, and what followed was an evil thing. Maybe she understood that Lute was riding a current he'd never be free of, but I doubt it. That woman's heart was as tight as a white-knuckled fist. She wanted to hurt him.

Lute Dross stayed stubborn, too, even while his mind was spinning like a whirlpool. He tried to get to his feet when Marlet's face was still as blurred as a winter moon behind the clouds. He reached up, gripped her blouse, coarse as field stubble to his fingers, and pulled. She told the sheriff he was attacking her, but that can't be true. Otherwise, his free hand wouldn't have been spread out on the sewing table—it would have been going for her throat. Lute was looking for balance, and Marlet stabbed him while he was down. Got those silver shears from somewhere in her dusty, sour skirts and plunged them into the web of his hand until they got hung up in wet bone and gristle.

Oh, I reckon he heard a song in his head then. Maybe he thought it was the baby crying, running a sweet tingle right up his arm. Maybe he thought it was Clare's pine-clean breath coming to him from wherever she was watching. Who knows what occupied the bit of his mind that wasn't soldered shut with pain. There probably ain't words for it. But Marlet should have gone ahead and killed him. That much I know. Instead of taunting him, wiping those bloody blades on his shirtsleeve and mocking him like a crow safe on a high, bare branch, she should have killed him. His death wouldn't have been the biggest sorrow—the boy was living by himself—and if he'd left the world then, crippled and dazed and washed pure in the memories of his mama and daddy, he wouldn't have been able to create the ruin that he did.

He had to hitch a ride to the hospital, you know. Once he fainted, Marlet dragged him out of the house and left him by her compost pile with a dirty bandage around his hand. It's no wonder he suffered from infection. But he never expressed any anger. Not once. When I saw him in the hospital, his face was as peaceful as a Jersey cow's. It was like he'd expected it to happen exactly as it had.

He was in the hospital for two or three days, but he didn't press charges. The sheriff knew Lute had been trespassing so he had to drop the matter. He did tell Lute and Marlet to stay clear of each other, however, and they both agreed, though Lute was so far into his fever that I doubt he remembered the promise.

After he was sent home, nobody saw him for several weeks. We were all tending to our gardens, and Colter was busy with his calves, so none of us took much time to worry about the boy.

He'd drawn up inside his den to heal, like a fox with a trap-cut foot. Except that Lute was past the point of just holing up. He stayed busy, real busy, inside that mind of his and out of it. The sheriff and I put together that much. Those last weeks of spring, while the Hardware River was rushing east with water the color of saw-blade rust, Lute was working on his wheel.

Seems he always wanted a waterwheel. His daddy thought it was pure foolishness—the river is slim as a creek up there, and the banks are too chipped and steep to hold any kind of mill. But it wasn't a mill that Lute wanted. Just a wheel, a handmade wheel that would spin with the weight of water. He'd imagined it for a long time and had filled an old chicken coop full of the oak, hickory, and locust he needed to build it. In fact, he must have started making the thing right after that big heron swooped onto his farm, before Marlet drew him off the mountain and away from his tools. Now, one-handed as he was, he finally had the will to finish it. He cut and greased an axle, squared the tracks, and shaped the wood for the rims. I've seen it, you know, and it's the craziest, most carefully constructed thing I've ever laid eyes on, designed to last a hundred years or more. Can't do anything but spin neither, just scoop and drop the water with a steady splash, like some sort of gurgling heart. That's the way it sounded to me, anyhow. Like a heart that was going to beat and squeeze until the world ended.

My guess is that the wheel triggered the rest. Lute knew the river the way he knew the veins on his arm, and he wanted to leave his mark. My wife believes that the bird had something to do with it, too. She takes Carla Tate's description of its cry— like a wailful sigh to the dead—on faith. And it's true, we saw plenty of signs that the bird had been living with Lute, right there in the house. Feathers and the queer, musty smell of its droppings were in almost every room. Looked as though its wing had gone bad or something. What's clear is that Lute finished the wheel in a few short weeks with the heron keening to him from indoors. He must've worked from dawn to dusk, the fever strumming a liquid tune in his head, his bad hand going stiff and swollen from holding the nails steady. He didn't bother to go back to the doctor, and his cousin in Stuart's Draft says she never heard from him after she drove him home from the hospital. No, that boy was hammering and sanding to get ready, and I'll be damned if he didn't know exactly what he was getting ready for.

All we can figure is that Clare brought the baby to Lute, lifted him right out of the cradle while Marlet was away at work. And since it was a Friday and there was a card game with the Peery boys at the Crossroads, it was two days before Marlet got home. She knew Clare was taking care of the child, so she didn't worry for a minute. She didn't begin worrying until she checked with her kin across the county, thinking that maybe her sister had gone off on a visit. Deep in her heart, though, way down under that barbed packet of ribs, I believe Marlet Keefe always knew where Clare and the baby had gone. But she couldn't stand to give rise to that belief. It would mean Lute had won, if only for a while. More than that, it would mean Lute had gotten what he wanted at her expense.

Finally, after making the sheriff check the bus stations as far away as Greensboro and Norfolk, she mentioned Lute's name. Sheriff wanted to know why in the wide world her sister would go to Lute Dross. You can imagine how that question set like acid in Marlet's ears. Just check on it, she told him, I've got my reasons. But the sheriff wasn't about to leap into the muddy ditch of an old grudge. By the time Marlet convinced him—don't ask me how she did it—it was well after dark.

Sheriff headed up the mountain early the following morning, and he asked me to go along because I knew Lute better than almost anybody. He didn't relish the thought of pulling into Lute's yard with a nervous deputy by his side. He figured the two of us could just talk to him real quick and be done with it. Until he saw the situation for himself, he didn't believe Clare Keefe could have gone anywhere near there.

We used my truck. But we had no sooner passed Colter's cornfield than we were forced to turn around. The road was washed plumb out. One of the runoff creeks had cut a deep red gash in the clay on its way to the Hardware, so there was no way we were climbing the mountain that day. Sheriff laughed a little—he's had to learn his patience—and said that old Lute couldn't have done a better job if he had used a pickaxe. I reminded him that Lute was pretty much one-handed these days, but staring at that roaring creek, I had to agree. The boy had the queerest luck.

We drove up the next afternoon. Had to borrow Jake Milliron's army surplus jeep to cross the gully, but this time the sheriff had two deputies ready to trail us on foot. Marlet was flat-out frantic by then, whirling through the basement of the courthouse with her skirts and fists in motion. She was raising some kind of hell, threatening to call in the state cops and all. The whole thing had started to gnaw at the sheriff like day-old coffee; I could see it on his face. He was beginning to expect the worst.

We checked the old farmhouse first. Lute's pickup was parked around back, cold and unused. There were cobwebs in the cab, and that bit of copper bracelet was hanging from the rearview mirror. The front porch was bare, so we went straight inside the house. And Lord have mercy, there was no way we could have been ready for what we saw.

I called for Lute a few times, but I could tell the place was empty. Not just empty, deserted—as though the air had seeped out and taken the warmth of blood with it. We searched every room, and that's when we began pulling the pieces together.

In the kitchen, somebody had set six fine china cups and saucers on the table. They must have belonged to Lute's mother, since they were gray with dust except where the tiny circles of fingertips had touched them. There were old linen napkins the color of dog's teeth, and I could see how Clare had been interrupted in the middle of planning some tea party. The oven was disconnected, but the knobs were turned as if the coil would heat up. A creased apron hung from one of the chairs, its ties halfway knotted. It seemed like that little gal might walk in any minute with her arms full of make-believe sugar and eggs.

Then there was Lute's room. Used to be his mama's, I guess, since the closets were full of mothballed dresses and shawls. But you have never seen a man's room done up like this one. Hair ribbons dangled in the windows, fluttering every time you moved or breathed. The sills were lined with marbles, dried flowers, and pieces of an old ivory comb—everything Clare had ever given him was on display. Some of his mama's dresses were laid out across the bed, unbuttoned, waiting to be taken off their hangers as though it was now time to wear them. I found a rag-lined basket on the floor and some bloodstains on the coverlet, most likely from Lute's bad hand, but we'll never know for sure. Most interesting to me was how we could tell that the bedroom was the only room in the house the bird hadn't been in. You could see the wheel from there too, right out the window between a pair of sycamores. The sheriff and I heard it while we were looking around—thump, thump, thump—sounding like a door that couldn't be closed.

When we were sure the house was empty, we headed back outside.

The sheriff was the one who found him. I'd wandered past the barn toward the west ridge, imagining how they'd all up and left. I was thinking that Lute had been smart as a whip. Staring across the mountaintop where the trees held the finest fringe of mist, I couldn't help but think that the land felt so peaceful. Before I knew it, though, the sheriff was calling to me from the riverbank, his voice deep and raspy the way it must have been in the army, telling me to get Weaver and Smith with the jeep. I did exactly what he said, didn't ask a single question, because I could tell from the ring of his words—sharp as struck brass—that things were bad.

We ran to the riverbank, the deputies and me, and it was as if the good Lord had struck us dumb. I had expected a drowning, so we'd loaded ourselves down with blankets, a tarpaulin, and some rope from the jeep. But I could feel my hands and arms go numb holding the stuff when I saw what had happened. That waterwheel, all dun-colored and smooth with some of the nail heads still shining in the sun, was spinning like a whirligig with Lute Dross tied up inside.

We couldn't tell if he was dead or alive. Sheriff had already taken a length of wood from behind the house, and it wasn't long before the four of us had braced the wheel and cut the boy down. He was lashed at the hands and ankles, and the way his wrists looked, we guessed he had been there at least one whole day, rolling around and around, going nowhere. The damnedest thing, though, was that the bird was tied in there with him, its neck broken, its feathers matted and torn. Christ, I remember standing up to my waist in water that smelled of clean-washed rock, with loose feathers whirling all around me, wondering what in hell had finally sprung that poor boy loose.

He'd tied himself in there, you see, and though he wasn't dead when we took him off the mountain, he didn't last the night. Exposure, the doctor said, and the infected hand had put a fair amount of poison in his blood. But I don't think the doctor cared to name what had actually killed him. It was too terrible to consider, since the boy had asked for so little the whole time he'd been alive. The bird was dead when he tied it to his body, we're sure of that. Its feathers weren't slick the way they should have been; they'd been petted clean. Lute couldn't stand to give it up, I guess. Clare had disappeared, the baby too, and even though Colter says he still expects their bones to come bobbing up in his pond, I think he's wrong. I don't know if I believe she's alive, mind you. Maybe she killed the bird or the baby died or maybe she just jumped in the river when she reckoned she couldn't live the way she and Lute imagined. I can see her above that rock-bottom stream with nothing but the billow of a moth-eaten dress to hold her high. The point is, she's gone, vanished, and the baby with her, like they never existed, as if they were only flickers in one of Marlet's well-stoked fires.

Teal slides back on his bench, his beer glass clasped like a torch between his hands. He's waiting for a response from me, his nephew, who's headed into the mountains to be alone with cold air and simplicity, and to teach a few scabby students. I say that I guess Cousin Lute could have been more patient. Teal shakes his head, his eyes registering a glint just short of anger.

No, *he says,* think about that bruise-purple ribbon around Lute's neck, how it twisted while he rolled inside that wheel, how he whispered to the bird lashed to his lap, how he whispered Honey, Honey, till he died. Think about how that wheel was straining to ride down the river when we got there, how it couldn't bear the load. Think about that, *he says as his hands rise from the glass in a glide of open palms.* Think about what that poor, forsaken boy was hoping to create.

BALLAD AND SADNESS

From the time I met him, I tried not to latch on. There is a power that falls like angels into this world, and this man bore it well, as naturally as the heat of his body. I was alone. The ferry was late. And, as the priest would tell me later, man's great flood is only water; woman's is hope.

I was on the dock at Kyleakin, Isle of Skye. It was raining, and I was wrapped in my poncho, shielded by its hood from the eyes of travelers who were smoking under the eaves of the Tourist Authority. My morning had been quiet and useless. After a breakfast of tea and toast, I'd left my rented room and hiked to Castle Moil, the squat, divided ruin that overlooks the channel between Skye and Scotland.

It took me half an hour to find a dry path and climb upward. The mist was heavy on the hills, the sun curtained and feeble. There was no sound except the breeze across the tower walls and the weak bleat of sheep. The sea was silver below me; the rock I laid a hand on was well hewn and square. As I looked west, I wondered how Evan would have felt about this land, the unfenced meadows thick with heather, and that was where I went wrong—lifting him into this context, imagining his flecked eyes on this uncultivated earth. The ferry must have sailed to Kyle of Lochalsh and back five times before the mist wove itself into fog, and I could no longer see the hills. When I descended, my hair was dripping with rain.

I was determined to be the first aboard the next ferry. Gazing past the hood of my poncho, I saw just one other backpacker and a pair of Germans with bikes. The rest of the passengers had cars, so when the crewman waved me aboard, I headed for the unsheltered bow, where I was sure I would be alone. Everyone at home had said I would leave—the doctors, the priest. Fear and sorrow were natural, they'd said. But they misunderstood my loss, I think. They thought I was only mourning for Evan. And though I'd been devastated by his crime, it was the farm that grieved me now. We had said we would till it together; we had sworn.

I'd been traveling like a spent bullet for two months, aimless, falling, as far from home as I could bear. Chinook and Lou were milking the herd. My second cousin was trying to buy me out. As far as anyone could tell, my departure was weakness, and the distance was the scope of my failure.

If Peter hadn't offered me that cigarette I might still be standing on the dark shore of some loch—a black slash beneath a spruce, a cold frozen shadow. But he joined me at the starboard rail, face to the wind, and made his offer. Soaked by the rain and bowed under the weight of my pack, I must have looked approachable.

His face hung before me like an etching or a print, a surface to study, not touch; his cheeks were flushed and planed, his eyes round and blue like a child's.

"Would you like a cig?" he asked.

"No." I shook my buried head, trying not to memorize the raw, worn skin of his hands. "Thanks."

He lit a hand-rolled cigarette, using my body as shelter. I could tell he hadn't shaved for a day or two, though he hardly needed it, and when he exhaled over my head, I saw that his teeth were slightly stained. He was tall for a Scotsman, very lean. "You'll be going to Fort William," he ventured. "On to London?"

"I'm going to Inverness," I said, "maybe farther."

"Ah, Inverness." He grinned, cigarette in his teeth. "I'll be traveling there, too, going to the fields."

"Which fields?" I asked.

"Oil, of course. There's nothing past Inverness but sheep and oil. I'm hoping for a rig."

I considered him more closely and made a guess. Eighteen? Nineteen? His neck was as pale as my wrist. He seemed proud of how far he'd come.

"Good luck," I said, seeing him shrunk by the surf of the North Sea.

He stubbed out his cigarette against the chipped gray rail and closed the butt in his hand. "Why don't we hitchhike together? To share rides?"

I looked at him in profile, the flush a little higher on his cheeks, his lips full and open. I thought I could afford to waste the train ticket in my belt, but I didn't know if I could afford the company.

"It's not something I do very much," I stammered.

"No worry," he said. "It's easy with two. We'll be there by nightfall."

I know now it was his fresh assurance that drew me to him like a moth to a flame.

"Peter," he said, extending a hand with short and dirty nails, "from Glasgow."

"Avery," I said, "from a place you've never heard of."

We tried to get a ride as soon as we got off the ferry but couldn't, so we started to walk. As the rain slowed down and the earth began to smell of root and stalk, a tune came into my head, a broken, nearly forgotten march. I was open again to the sifting breeze of the hills. The late sun was a warm hand on my throat.

He began to tell me about his father and the railway and the dole. He was nonchalant about his poverty; that was Glasgow. But he was surprised to hear about my farm, about the work I did on my own.

"A dairy? I've met only students from America," he said, looking skeptical. "I wouldnae thought."

"I've been to school," I said. "The farm's in the family. I just stayed with it."

"So you're up early in the morning, tending from dawn till dark?" I could tell he was teasing; he couldn't imagine me in the cold and the slop.

"Yes," I said, "when it's my turn. I know more about ground nutrients and butterfat and mortgages than I need to."

"Well enough," he said, turning away, laughing. "I cannae stand a cow."

Then he asked about my family. He had a mum who slapped him when he was smart and a sister, Maura, who wanted to be a nurse. What about me? Was my da a good worker? I told him my parents were dead, slowly dead, and that I missed them.

I also told him—my head was light when I said it—that I'd once run the farm with my brother.

"He's not married?"

"No." I felt my chest tighten like a bow. "He's in prison."

He didn't follow that trail. He must have guessed it was my reason for being here. Finally a grocer stopped to give us a lift. After we both jumped in, Peter did the talking while I tried to fall asleep on the dusty back seat of the car. Thirty kilometers later, when we were left at a crossroads, Peter said that he'd told the driver that I was his sister.

"You're fair enough," he said. "Got the same length of hair."

I suppose I knew then what would happen. I could smell it like chalk in poor soil. He would want to sleep with me, and I would let him. He was attractive and younger by a dozen years. His body would be strong. But I would feel dead-handed and empty, further broken when it was done.

We got no more rides. I shared the few biscuits I had in my pack, though without much pleasure. The night promised to be mild, but the fingers of my once callused hands were stiff with cold as we ate. There was only one voice in my ears—my own. One choice.

I didn't know how to introduce him to my mistaken heart, so I let him lead. The sun fell quickly past the blue-stroke mountains, fraying our shadows like rags, but Peter had no problem finding shelter. At dusk, we left the road for a path marked by a cairn that could have been new or legendary. After a few steps, we pushed through a hedge and followed a small stream into a grove of stunted trees. The ground had been pressed flat by the hot, panting flanks of sheep. It was a good place to sleep, but not to dream, I thought. The rough land around us was as steep and solid as the rim of a bowl, its sustenance camouflaged with gorse and thorn.

I gathered straw and what wood I could find for a fire, then filled a tin pot for tea. Peter raised his tent with a soft recital of curses, and I found myself once more aware of the warm, unwashed smell of his body, coarse but lasting. I imagined the icy joints of an offshore rig, the harsh, trusting scramble of a crew. I decided that Peter, with his lithe build and abiding spirit, would manage well at sea.

We settled by the fire in the dark. The tea was smoky and rich, like broth on my tongue. I had long since stopped talking. I was too far away—from my roving herd, my sweet clover farm, the ferment of my silos. A growing apprehension settled in my limbs. Pray that he's awkward, I told myself. Know that he'll forget.

He didn't speak either. Instead he began to play the harmonica, cupping it in his large-knuckled hands. And what he played sounded like sadness, I thought, an answer to the lark's last call, a harmony for stones.

I hadn't even seen him pull the instrument from his pack. My eyes were on the red, crumbling coals and the air above them, blurred and wavering. His music rose easily and clear. It was nothing like memory. Evan and I hadn't spoken in those tones. Even our laughter didn't have that range. If it had, he might have told me how he felt about that boy. I might have cherished him even more and protected him enough to betray him when I should have.

But he had treated me—his little sister—like a child. I thought of Evan in the walnut tree outside my window, howling with the peacocks, shouting *Lazy Avery, get your sweet ass out of bed*. Or Evan yelling at me over the churn of the tractor, insisting that I stay out of the toolbox, away from repairs. Sometimes those are the only sounds I hear—his demands, his pleas.

"It's my grandad's song," Peter said, wiping his lips on a sleeve. "I hope you don't mind."

I shook my head, eyes closed.

"He was from Oban, Campbell country." Peter coaxed me a little, leaning on his words. "Where he was famous for his songs."

"Is he alive?" I asked.

"No. He left the world an old, old man."

"He's lucky then."

I heard Peter's boots scrape the ground.

"Do you wish your brother was dead?" he asked suddenly. "Is that what you're thinking?"

"Yes," I said, lifting my head and staring as hard as I could. "I think about that all the time."

He raised his hands and played on. Long songs, slow and rocking like the ripples of a pond, songs with pitched refrains. He stopped once to tell me how to move my feet, but I told him I was hopeless at such things. The rest of his songs were ballads, plaintive in their rise and fall. Before long, he gave up pausing between each one.

It was the darkness that made me sing. Not out loud, but in the hollow of my mouth. I didn't hide my face; Peter might have thought I was crying. So I let my lips move, spelling my silence with pressed air. I might have been Evan mocking the peacocks, a wide-mouth strut as they preened.

"I'll stop if you're tired."

"No, no it's lovely," I said. "True to the night."

"Perhaps," he said, removing his glasses, looking plain and slightly harsh across the fire. "The Highlands are grief without mourning, my grandad used to say."

"Except for their history."

"Ah, no," he said, laughing quietly. "We've suffered no more than most. In my da's house, the whole family sings. Together we make our greatest noise . . . for the pubs and around."

"And when you're alone?"

He gazed at his hands, the harmonica like a hilt across his palm. "It's just me and my harp. No need for words then."

I smiled at him, seeing once more how brave he was at being on his own, how he'd managed to escape the black-rock plunge of failed loyalty. His confidence was restless, but certain.

"I could teach you the verse. I mean, the part a lady might sing."

"No," I said, pushing a twisted stick into the fire. "I'd like to go to sleep."

I did what I'd promised myself. I undressed openly, freeing my tangled brown hair from its bands and pins. The air was strangely warm under the gaunt, barkless trees, and it fingered my legs lightly, like a veil. Maybe it was the fire, or the fleece of my own daring, but even in my nakedness, I didn't shiver.

"You don't mind sharing the tent?" I asked. My eyes were heavy on the sweep of his shoulders.

"No." He was rolling a cigarette. "But I'll be staying with the night awhile."

"Fair enough," I said. "Good night."

"Aye. You too."

He had turned from me when I stripped, and had kept to himself, his legs stretched out past the fire. I could smell the burn of his cigarette, fresh and live against the sourness of sheep dung and mud. I slid into the dull shell of the tent on my back, head first. He was right: night was a comfort to the wayfarer, a sanctuary, a reprieve. But only if the journey had a cause, I thought. If the wander were a thread.

He played his harmonica again, more deeply and softly than before, and no matter what I told myself, I couldn't stop believing he was playing it for me. The notes reached and quivered; each phrase was followed by his voice, a steady tenor so rich with accent his words were unintelligible in the wind. But I could feel what he was singing just the same: *What is lost is not forgotten, what is treasured will tarnish slow.* He sang with quiet conviction and simple abandonment, although I sensed that his sorrows had been passed down to him or borrowed; his own spirit was barely scuffed. He bent and curled the notes as if they were made of gold leaf.

He joined me later, the moon lacing his body with shadows that stroked his flesh like a signature, the hum of his songs still present in his smoky breath.

We were clumsy, terribly so. But neither of us expected more. He was mostly silent, his hands wrapped in my hair, and I was thankful for that, taken beyond the fetal curl of memory. The ground was unresilient beneath me.

He slept quickly, carelessly, breathing in childlike contentment. His lips had parted, wet and helpless, just as Evan's had when we shared a bedroom as kids and kissed each other before our prayers. I studied the loose fling of his limbs. So much could be hidden in intimacy, so much sheltered in a sprawl.

The priest said that Evan wanted me to find him, wanted me to step into that tenant cottage and see him, bare from waist to ankle, his overalls coiled and glinting, embracing the limbs of the Hatcher boy. The young boy's face was pressed against the mattress like a loaf; his eyes were open like keyholes.

Evan came to my room after sunset. *Trust me,* he'd said. *You know me too well to be scared.* But what did I know? That my brother was a good man, a fair man, the only man I loved enough to lie for? He had asked me to hold fast and say nothing.

So someone else caught him with an even younger boy. The child had hair like combed cotton and hands no larger than cards, and when I saw his round face pinched tight above his collar, I knew I had failed. I should have clasped my brother's fingers and splintered them in love. I should have turned him in. The priest was right: there is only time for one kiss of betrayal.

I had shut myself in the farmhouse during the trial, trying to balance our accounts. But I was able to do nothing more than feed the peacocks and call up his look of cut longing, the way Evan's twist of desire had gone silver in his eyes.

Peter turned to his side as I watched, rolling his back from the fabric of the sleeping bag as if it were a mold. I wanted to touch the ivory crest of his spine; I wanted to feel the bone. Running my fingers along the arch of his pelvis, I imagined the endless spring of his body, the flex that would take him into manhood and stiffness and waste. My hand eddied the air above him; my skin was damp and musky like his own. He was as far from me as Evan's sculpted child had been from him— hairless, alabaster, innocent.

But when I turned Peter toward me, his arms and legs pliant in sleep, my hair like a curtain on his ribs, the bright sheen I had imagined disappeared. His lips seemed scaly and cracked, the neck thin. At that hour, the hollows of his chest were almost waiflike. And I wanted to see his ugliness because I couldn't bear it in myself, in my blood. I hadn't stopped Evan. I had wanted to believe that we could wash our family hands. I knew now that they could never be clean. Not with water, not with time.

My anger became a white dome inside my skull. Tears filled its cup. I had wished many times that Evan was dead, wished he had gotten sick or been killed before I discovered the terrible vault of his heart. But his face was behind my hot eyelids, his step in my pulse. I would have to live with him, if not for him— constant, bittersweet thief that he was—though even the priest had been less giving. Condemn him, he said, damn him completely. From the dry ash will come new flame.

With the grief still on my lips, I bent over Peter, left a moist petal of touch on his shoulder. He had given me the best truth he knew. I drew the rough blanket over his body and mine.

As I lay back, calmed by the sight of this stranger, I thought of the farm where someday I'd sow the wet, red clay on my own. Until then, I would cross an entire country—maybe aim for the eastern coast, where the mackerel and haddock flashed toward the north and the villages were filled with the stink of catch and haul. Or visit the fields of Fife, where, at this time of year, they were cutting and threshing grain and the calves were ready to wean. I'd go somewhere beyond the mountains, somewhere further, I knew, where the spiral of Peter's ballads would turn in my mind like a sea-whipped breeze—the notes ceaseless, the words age-rounded, the longing as bold as the lost promise of my brother's face.

THE FIELD
OF
LOST SHOES

I met her at New Market just like she asked. She thought it would look good to her husband that way and good to me, the road scholar, the able guy. She had promised she wouldn't pull any punches; this would be an honest get-together. We really would meet halfway. She would bring Timothy along too, she said. For her protection and mine.

It took me four hours to get as far as Lexington. I'd taken a five-mile run at dawn, a crazy, beautiful thing to do in east Tennessee, and had some coffee after my shower, while the sky was still lead-colored and cold. But I wasn't hungry. All I could think about was Ellen having lunch in the restaurant on Afton

Mountain, explaining to her son how they were going to eat ice cream, then drive into the valley for some history.

I hadn't seen Ellen in three months, not since I'd packed my books and files and left for East Tennessee State University, my first teaching job. Ellen had been proud of me—was still proud of me, I thought, if you could say pride slid in that direction. And though she had written to me every Wednesday, while her husband Denny was teaching his seminar on Jefferson Davis, what I felt behind her words was only the very edge of things. *It's over, it's never over.* Her letters said both, written as they were in the hard varnished smell of Denny's study. So when she called me, a reckless thing to do, and said, *Meet me at New Market battlefield, it makes sense, you could be there,* I said yes, even though I knew it could go wrong. She was bringing Denny's son; she was playing Denny's wife. Ellen and I could talk all we wanted, but her husband would still be there, casting shadows as dark and heavy as his moods.

And yet, Ellen had made me feel exhilarated, poorly aimed and powerful the whole time we were together. So she didn't have to sound desperate to convince me of anything. I'd be there. If she wanted to stake something—her time, her marriage, the wide eyes of her son—on seeing me again, that was her gamble. I didn't have anything to lose.

I'd never been to the battlefield, though I'd driven by it plenty of times. Ellen seemed to think it would be the perfect place for me—for us—because I was a historian just like her husband. But the Civil War was not one of my interests, a fact she would have taken into account if she'd been thinking clearly. Appalachia was more my line—the history of the mining companies, oral folklore, etc. Denny was the political buff, whether she realized it or not.

The New Market Visitors Center stood out among the modest

farms near the highway, as proud as a mausoleum on a backlit hill. Its slanted stone walls were so stern and confident that I parked my car a respectful distance away. I knew that the South had celebrated one of its last victories here, a win fashioned from true and mythical Rebel strengths. The Confederates had been outnumbered and outgunned. Lee was across the mountains. Stonewall Jackson was dead. But the Yankees had been turned back, the farmers left free to cultivate their wheat and corn.

I stepped through the double doors, and a young woman with badly frosted hair offered a crisp, metallic-smelling brochure in exchange for my donation. The woman barely glanced at me; I might have been one tourist in a million, except that the building looked empty. I knew Ellen would be late—she enjoyed the drama of delay—so I decided to go ahead and see the sights. There was no way we could miss each other in all this hush.

The exhibit hall was carefully organized. I heard marching music, then cavalry hooves, then cannon fire. Miniature men rushed frantically across miniature terrains. As I studied the maps that traced Confederate strategy in bold color, it was easy to see how victory had been preserved for more than a century. Forget the fact that Sheridan burned his way down the valley before the summer was over. The Yankees had been whipped before that, right here.

I'd seen everything but the feature film by one o'clock, and since I thought Timothy might like to see the film with me, I went back to the lobby to wait. Ellen would appreciate the fact I'd thought of her son. Then again, Ellen tended to take such things for granted. What I probably wanted to do was reassure her, let her know I remembered her and respected her and loved her. The fact that Timothy was with her only increased my care.

The lobby was quiet and wood-trimmed and topped with a cathedral ceiling; it reminded me of church. There was a stained-glass window—a blue, gray, and red tribute to the battle that stretched along the southern wall. The glass was thickly textured, and the colors were more vivid than any I'd ever seen in churches, where the windows tell a simpler story.

New Market was a matter of pride and romance, and romance was something Virginians understood, just like their Scotch-Irish fathers. It was an excess they enjoyed. An old claw-hammer banjo player I once knew had put it like this: *My dead daddy played best and his daddy played better before him, I done lost the good songs behind me.*

I was looking at the window, watching the crossbar flags absorb the clear afternoon light, when the janitor interrupted me. It occurred to me later that maybe he wasn't a janitor, maybe he was the curator or an eccentric academic. I hadn't seen anyone except the frost-haired woman; I wondered who ran the place. This old fellow was pushing a broom across the smooth slate floor as he talked.

"Brings tears to your eyes, doesn't it," he said, swinging his broom close enough to brush my heels. "I've been here a long time and I still cry."

"It's impressive," I said.

"Have you been outside yet? Seen Bushong's farm and the old turnpike? The house still has holes in it."

"I'm waiting for someone," I said. "Maybe we'll take a look when they get here."

"I can't recommend it enough. Nothing like it in the whole war. Those boys marching up from Lexington. Nothing like it at Bull Run or the Wilderness either. I've seen them all. I know."

I guessed he was in his sixties, a small man with leathery hands like you'd expect to find on a farmer. The skin on his face was slack in places, especially around his jaw, but his eyes were sharp, though a little bloodshot. Once he dropped a hand into his pocket and pulled out a big white-faced watch. I couldn't shake the feeling that he was more sophisticated, or maybe just crazier, than he seemed.

"I noticed you were from Tennessee." His head wobbled on his neck. "The Volunteer State. Bloody Murfreesboro."

It bothered me that he'd noticed my car. It shouldn't have mattered, but the old man made me nervous. He swept the floor with huge, shoving strokes, then shuffled away, his eyes on the ceiling beams that were speckled with refracted light. He clenched his jaw as if he were counting something in his head, and suddenly he was gone, shut off by a paneled door marked Private. His absence brought the hush back to the lobby, and I was alone again, hungry, jittery, wondering if I should laugh or break into a sweat. I was in an elegant shrine to a little piece of war famous for charging boys into men, and I was shivering.

Ellen drove up a few minutes later. She was in her car, a boxy Ford hatchback, and my heart went as flat as a crushed can when I saw it. I remembered the last time I'd seen her, the day before I left town. I'd gone into the A&P to buy some tape, and there she was, choosing grapefruit. We'd already said our good-byes. Yet I found myself close behind her, gazing down on her pale, bare neck, thinking that she was still young and beautiful. I wanted to watch her, secretly, for as long as I could. Holding my breath, I collected a memory.

This time, I waited for her. I wasn't going to try to fool Timothy, but I wasn't going to make it worse for him either, not by rushing up to his mother with my eyes bright and my hands whirling. Ellen was wearing a chocolate brown skirt and high heels and a creamy, tailored blouse that emphasized her breasts. Her dark hair was pulled back in a French twist, and she walked as if she were very self-assured, like the lawyer or broker she sometimes wished she could be. Timothy trailed behind her with her purse in his hands. She let him handle the donations while she headed straight for me, her shoes sounding hard and fast on the slate. I smelled the gardenia in her perfume before she stopped.

We looked at each other for several seconds, both of us wondering who was going to set the first stakes.

"You can hug me, you know," Ellen said, pressing on her lower lip.

I stepped forward and kissed her on the cheek, but the hug was all wrong. I hooked her too high across the back and pulled her to my side as if her body were shapeless. Sometimes, awkwardness can be sweet. Ellen had said that on the first afternoon we found ourselves in bed, though I'd always wondered if she really believed that she overlooked such things.

"Hello, Tim," I said, waving to him over Ellen's shoulder. "How've you been?" He didn't answer, just stood there clutching his mother's purse and two brochures as if he wanted to be somewhere else. He was a thin boy with freckles and reddish-blonde hair—a small, wiry version of his father, except his eyes, which were round and hazel, like Ellen's.

"He's a little shy," Ellen said. "But he's like Denny, he'll be completely absorbed in detail before long." She put her arm through mine and guided me toward her son, her head tilted at an angle that was supposed to be coy. I hadn't expected this, not a frontal assault. I thought I'd hauled myself north for understanding, the sweet resolution of loss.

I held out my hand and Timothy shook it with a quick, formal snap. I could see that he didn't remember me, though he'd met me once when I'd dropped off some papers for Denny. He turned to stare at the high wall of stained glass, deferring to his mother. Ellen had always described him as an obedient child, a child she adored until she decided it was selfish of her to depend on him.

"Well, you were here first." Ellen raised her hands in an animated shrug. "Where do we start?"

"The movie," I said, remembering my plans. "It gives the overview. Then there are the exhibits and the battlefield. I think that's the way to go."

"Sound okay?" Ellen bent to remove Timothy's jacket.

"Yes ma'am," he said.

"Fine. Professor Marlowe, you're in charge." She spoke with a hint of a giggle, but I saw the skin around her eyes go tight, and realized what her lips would look like without the bronze gloss of lipstick—thin, drawn, vaguely worried. She could say what she pleased, but I wasn't in charge. And neither was she.

The theater contained about two dozen seats. A large white button on the wall allowed us to start the film when we were ready. Ellen glanced around, then excused herself. "Y'all go ahead," she said, smiling for Timothy and vamping for me. "I'll be back when I can."

I let Timothy choose our seats, a decision that loosened him up a little, and we settled in the front row before the house lights went down. He saved a seat for Ellen between us.

The movie warmed up with fife and drum, the same tune that heralds every Civil War battle as something distinctly American, innocent and brash from the beginning. At New Market the fife announced the coming of the VMI cadets, a thirty-seven-mile march by schoolboys who saved the day. I noticed how the music was setting me up for a tragic thrill, the gut-tight rush before sorrow.

While the narrator explained the Southern troop shortage and the need to defend the turnpike, I slipped down in my seat, my legs stretched out toward the screen. Before long I was the same height as Timothy, who was also slumped, face lifted, eyes open and rapt. "Hey," I said, as a few bearded actors and prancing horses staged Imboden's advance cavalry raid, "this is pretty good."

"Yeah," he said. "I can't wait to see it again."

I understood then why Ellen was missing. She knew her son; she'd raised him. She knew he'd stare at a screen filled with advance and retreat for at least an hour. Maybe she'd told him to stay put, maybe she'd planned this. I could feel myself getting tense, so I refocused my eyes to let it pass. Above me, the screen was covered with the sepia-toned portraits of Yankee commanders, square-faced, deep-eyed, and grim.

I reached across the empty seat and touched the boy's small elbow. "I'm going to check on your mom," I whispered. "You sit tight. I'll be back for the good part." He nodded without looking at me, but I knew I'd been acknowledged because he hadn't flinched when I touched him. I drew in my legs and left on tiptoe, preparing to sidle out of certain confrontation.

She was sitting on a blue padded bench in the hallway, smoking a cigarette, which would be her excuse—that she needed to relax. But the Ellen I'd known smoked only when she drank. Cigarettes were part of an old pose, she'd told me, something she'd picked up from her roommate at Hollins. She winked when she saw me and tapped her ashes into the silver basin of a water fountain. I felt as if I'd been waved off the dance floor by the homecoming queen.

"You're missing a pretty good show," I said.

"So are you," she said, swinging her knees to one side to give me her best profile. "Besides, I'm tired."

"Maybe I should go back to Timmy then. I just thought you were lost."

She laughed, and I noticed that her lipstick was fresh and perfect. She really could be lovely, a fact brought home by the neat curve of her throat. I remembered her startled blush when I lifted that A&P grapefruit from her hand. She hadn't had a single second to think. She'd reached up to touch my breastbone, her eyes a soft liquid brown. Then she'd recovered, her pupils going blank and hard.

"Don't go anywhere," she said. "Timmy's fine."

"So what's the rest of your plan?" I asked. "Should we talk? How are you?"

I'm not much for sarcasm, so my concern—and that's what it was—surprised her. Sincerity tended to confuse Ellen because Denny considered himself a polished wit, an ironic intelligence with an acid tongue; he always undercut her. I wasn't so predictable, or so sure of myself.

"I miss you," she said, dousing her cigarette in the fountain. "It's not easy to say that. I feel silly."

"I think about you too. There aren't any beautiful wives in Johnson City." I smiled, trying to revive our best joke, the one about ourselves.

"You're sweet," she said, "but let's just stick to today."

"Here I am."

"I know. I pretend to leave Denny every day," she said. "Now I remember why."

It was familiar ground, an indulgent tangle of wishes and denials we had both wanted a few months earlier. Ellen's voice became softer, more tentative, and she turned to face me. I saw that she was prepared to worry the idea of leaving Denny as though it were a shiny stone in her hand that had the power to conjure my resolve and bring me back to her.

"You don't have to flatter me," I said. I sat down beside her and reached around her waist. "I'd rather not be full of regrets. The film will be over soon. Is there some real trouble somewhere?"

"Don't worry about Timmy. He loves places like this. He can take care of himself."

I raised my hand to trace the edge of her chiffon collar, my fingertips tingling. "I don't want to confuse him, that's all."

"He could use some confusion. So could you." She kissed me hard then, her hands touching my knees, her weight coming behind the push of her lips and tongue. I felt the blood heat up in my chest and thighs.

"You want to know the truth," she said, breaking away to let me know she was kissing me out of anger as much as anything else. "The truth is, my car is going to break down this afternoon, and Timmy and I are staying over, and I'm going to be with you tonight. That's my so-called plan."

She looked at me, her forehead set and smooth, her mouth pressed closed as if she had given me a choice and was waiting for my answer. In or out. Yes or no. But there wasn't a choice. Part of me wanted the night at Howard Johnson's, the long, muffled night down the hall from where Timmy would be sleeping in a room littered with candy wrappers and comics, whatever would appease. Ellen would be warm and slippery, at her best, most fragile peak. And I would feel it again, the thin, dark plumb line of taking a turn that cannot be retraced. There was depth to that; it could be a night I'd never forget. But it could also be a night without end, a deed without boundary. Because Ellen would want it again and again, maybe only in miniature, maybe only on the phone, but she would consider it a promise wrapped around a core of hope, and she wouldn't let it go. Not for a very long time.

"It'll just hurt you," I said.

"Hurt me? Who said I wanted anything more than a good screw?" She stood up then, her hips tucked forward as she threw back her head and glared. "You don't want to understand, do you?"

"Ellen, honey. I said that wrong." I put a hand on her hip, taking a chance. "Let me tell the truth. It'll hurt me. I love you, but it can't work."

"Who said anything about love?" She swallowed between her words. "I'm keeping this simple."

"You know it's not simple. And Timmy's here now, I'm not going to involve him." I ran my hand down her arm, trying to soothe, trying to regain the woven feeling in my skin.

"Timmy's not your decision, you bastard. How dare you make him an excuse. I suggest one thing, and you ruin it, you ruin it for us all."

She was crying then, and so was I, my eyes burning, my throat feeling round and hollow. I wanted to hold her. I wanted to make love to her for a hundred dark and separate nights. But the truth was there beneath the light, powdery makeup that had softened on her cheeks. My Ellen was old—not so much in body as in heart. She wasn't prepared to love me or leave Denny. She'd resorted to wheedling revenge because that was what she knew; it was Denny's own medicine in triple dose. She had stepped out of bounds with me, but she would never stay there. Because that would leave her with nothing—not her son or her simmering, necessary anger.

"I can't stretch things out," I said. "It's wrong."

She screamed at me then, cursing what she called my horny morality. Before she left, she asked me why I'd come, what I thought I'd get besides her ass. And I told her what I suppose I had known since my run through the football stadium early that morning when I made my legs carry me high into the bleachers while my guts knotted and rocked. I'd come to get what I deserved, to take the kicks and blame I'd truly earned.

I watched her stumble up the carpeted stairs, her sobs buckling against the wall behind me. I thought first of the old man with the broom, wondering what he would think of such behavior. He would probably find us profane—whispering and shouting about love in a hall of valor and death. Then I thought of Timmy, alone with his cannons and heroes. I knew Ellen would be back before long. But for now, because of the vagaries of quarrel and trust, Timmy was mine.

He had started the movie a second time, so when I walked into the flickering theater, I heard the shrill fife and witnessed the wild ride of Imboden's cavalry once more. The horses swirled like leaves on a biting wind. It occurred to me that Timmy didn't like silence. He could handle being alone, but silence—a confirmation of his mother's bitter eyes—was too much for him. I imagined him pressing the white button with his oval palm, evading the strained voices in the hall, edging away.

"Hey," I said, settling next to him. "Your mom's not feeling well. How's the movie?"

"It's good," he said.

"All right. What do you say we go outside and see it live. Rude's Hill, the orchard, the places where the artillery was set up. Until your mom feels better."

"But you missed the movie," he said, reminding me of my promise.

"That's okay," I said. "I've heard the story before."

The famous bottleneck between Smith Creek and the rise of the Blue Ridge Mountains was planted in wheat, and except for the plateau of the interstate, the battlefield was so featureless that I became disoriented. Timmy found a plastic-framed map, and together we scouted the land for points of interest. Though I expected Ellen to return at any moment, straight-lipped and firm in her claim to what was hers, I was able to relax a little. Timmy was chest-high and talkative; he seemed to like me because of what we currently had in common.

It was his idea to walk to the farm. The Bushong house was maybe a half mile from where we stood, surrounded by wheat and perfect four-board fences. There weren't any sidewalks or trails; the Historical Commission seemed to hope no one would take the trouble. But I decided that a couple of visitors wouldn't bother anyone. And Timmy was right. The Bushong farm was where the action was, or had been.

I swung him over a creosote-stained gate. He laughed out loud, his mouth wide open in the air. Denny wasn't a large man—Ellen said his presence never felt physical—and I wondered how Timmy saw his father, if he thought of him as old and brilliant, the kind of man people listened to, a man who got his way. I knew I must seem very different to him with my scuffed jacket and flyaway hair, a young man without certainty on his face. And it suddenly became clear to me that Ellen had brought Timmy along for his own protection, not hers or mine. She'd brought her son to save him from the lies, the webs she'd have to weave back home in Charlottesville. Watching him run into the field with wheat up to his elbows and the beat of an imaginary drummer on his lips, I knew what cruelty was. Cruelty was forgetting the delicate paper heart of a child. Cruelty was dropping the shield.

"This wouldn't have been so easy with the cannons and bullets going," I said. "Even the Yankees were pretty good shots."

Timmy hoisted a pretend rifle on his shoulder. "It would've

been noisy," he said, "like the movie." He imitated the whistle of an artillery shell, his freckled cheeks exploding with the shrapnel of sound.

"And scary. There's nowhere to hide."

"Would you have been scared, Mr. Marlowe?" He glanced up at me, then ran forward a step, two steps, waiting for my answer. I saw that Denny had been the fatherly model for a few things. Glory, heroism, certain historical hurrahs. "Yes," I said, "I probably would have been. I wouldn't want to die."

"I wouldn't be scared." He slowed his choppy pace to fall in line with mine.

"That's the thing about this place," I said, laughing a little. "The Yankees attack. And the South wins because of the perfect courage of boys."

I looked past the clean white farmhouse toward the orchard where teenagers had plugged a busted line and kept the bluecoats from spilling through. "We don't fight like this anymore. Nowadays, we fight almost blind. In jungles."

"I could go to VMI," Timmy said. "My father almost did."

"Would you like to?"

"When I'm older," he said. "I'm only ten."

"And I'm almost thirty." I leaned against the barnyard fence. "An old man."

"My mom got mad at you, didn't she?"

I looked into his round, gold-flecked eyes, discovering what every parent must know a thousand times over, that sons and daughters are aware of more than their tongues can say.

"Yep," I said.

"But you like my mom, don't you?" His words folded into a shy stutter. "You don't hate her now?"

"I don't hate her. To tell you the truth," and he seemed to deserve this much, his face so frail with expectation, "I probably like your mom too much. That makes it even harder."

He tried to seem serious for a moment, but he was soon pulling himself onto the orchard fence, aiming his fingers toward Yankee territory. "I love her," he said. "More than anything."

Watching him fire distracted blanks, I knew that Ellen and I had wrought something dangerous and alive. She was wholly prepared to draw her son into our maelstrom, to teach him the truth of the whirling, sucking love that could not hold. But what he already knew was sufficient for any boy.

"Timmy," I said, "let me tell you about the fight for this orchard."

"What," he said, swinging a narrow leg across the fence. "I learned lots from the movie. Like how they were only a few years older than me. Like how they won the whole thing."

"It happened out there," I said, pointing vaguely beyond the bare apple trees. "When the boys, the cadets, were heading toward the ridge, they ran into a swamp of mud because it had been raining hard, like in the movie."

He tilted his head—curious and impatient, just like his mother.

"They hit the mud and stuck. Some of them died there. Some of them made it through barefoot, they lost their shoes and boots and everything. But they didn't stop. They kept running and firing and swimming through mud until they silenced the cannon." I looked across the fence into his well-combed reddish hair. He was fidgeting a little. I dropped my hands to my sides. "It's amazing when you think about it."

"I could do that," he said. "Even if I wasn't really a cadet."

"I know you could," I said. "You'd have to be very brave, but you could do it."

He smiled then, a big toothy smile, and took off through the twisted orchard without waiting for me, rushing forward with sounds and ghosts of his own. And I wished I could explain everything to him—his mother, my broken feelings, myself—

before he ran. I wished hard for the impossible: that I could tell him about the inevitable douse of failure and the struggle to capture even one inch of our lives. But I didn't. Given the burdens of my age and the buoyancy of his, I could only follow his launch into the fife melody of a lie, watch him run with its simple purity across that field, gold and green and now untrodden, barely led by the twin barrels of our long, misshapen shadows.

A SEEMING
MERMAID

His chair was angled under the corner of a badly stained table. He'd been sitting there, talking about her for hours. Raising his hands before his face, he'd hold his square-end fingers straight and say her name while the light winked between his burnished knuckles. To me, those hands looked like cedar heart. He described her as if she was an unfolding scarf or a winter swan or a twice-cut prism, pausing often to see if I objected. I had heard people speak about their lovers before, but it had been a long time since I'd heard a man use such language—so strenuously, so honestly. Yet the words that were leaping from Cole's mouth now were too personal and arabesque to make sense. He wasn't able to capture her.

In fact, I already understood how poetry could fail a human tongue. A man once called me an angel in cotton cloth, a woman once said I was divine in a closed room. And though there had been a time when I might have been considered a gauzy chanteuse, my memories of actual affection were cold whispers. I had drifted so far from the persistent, salty dribble of love, I almost had to wonder if the memory of it was enough.

But Cole was like Atlas, lifting the burden of his own love upon his shoulders.

He had cared for Anna in a delicate, restrained way, something she had cherished because it was recognizable. He'd been working at the botanical gardens—dirty work, he said, elbows and palm-lines oiled with black earth. He was unskilled labor hunched behind the chief botanist, a plastic sack of peat on his shoulder. He did what he was told—plucked, fingered, rooted, sprayed. He watched. He peered. He waited. It was an easy place in which to be simple, and he wanted it that way, maybe for as long as a year.

And when he threw up those limber, absorbent hands, remembering how it was before Anna came, he recreated those days of mist and chlorophyll, time unfurling like a fern. He had removed himself from worry. He was living under a filtered sun. He had become so nonessential. His hair was thick with interior dew.

He would call her a ferret, a tern, a Canadian lynx. He would open his mouth and mimic the sounds.

Anna was beautiful. I'd seen her at the market, wearing a square alpaca cape the color of bitter cocoa. She made herself tall the way she held her refined head, never stooping to the vegetables and fruit. Sweet bell peppers, chives, eggplant; she could carry anything in her arms and look graceful. Her profile dovetailed with her age. Her cheeks were serious, her nostrils flexed. I thought to myself when I saw her dark eyes—too small for innocence, too fixed for Botticelli—that here was a woman without waste. Her throat was unadorned, her brass earrings rocked. But even if I had known who she was, I wouldn't have felt the vacant joy of appreciation as she raised her nimble hand to the scale. Shallots. Fresh basil. My bare skin prickled. Her poise was like an animal's crouch and spring.

He described her as mountain laurel—white-blossomed, shiny-leaved, weathered—then met my gaze unevenly at the table, his chair like a prow askew, fists heavy on his face. He wanted to complete her, be unwitched, discover where he'd hit bottom. He stared at me—his hair spooled with the colors of a pheasant's wing—and asked what he did wrong, would he always fail.

He first saw her in the orchid room. Slender, a long jacket the texture of frosted moss, alone, a purse comfortable against her thigh. From where he stood, roots were grazing across her throat, waxy and drenched. Orchids hung and brushed against her.

He told me he would dream it again and again: *Anna in the orchid room, her jacket hothouse glass. She trembles like the lip of a cymbidium. The flowers are bleeding red and gold, blooming and wilting in a chorus of motion. He is there, between the* Odonto-glossum *and the* Phalaenopsis, *but she does not see him, and he does not move. Even when a white-veined petal falls at her feet, he is still. Not frozen, but still. His scent is undetectable. The fallen petal, feeble as a wayward child, quivers, but she doesn't touch it. If she did, her hand would drop below the horizon of her handbag, past the clay pots and agile stems, and she might touch him. His eyes would spread with oil, venous blood.*

Inappropriate love, I said. Golden barge on the Nile.

The multiple lines on his face would not accept this.

She had returned to the gardens whether he dreamed her or not. His hands were sandy, pebble-chafed from tropical feeding and care. She said she was no longer married and her child was lost to her, bracketed by its father. She wore a sweater that, from a watery distance, might have been a bronze fish scale. She said she envied his work. Green and green and green.

He'd cooked her a meal. Sautéed veal, mousse, Vivaldi. You knew what you were doing, I said. You can't put up a sheik's tent without expecting Bedouin hooves on the wind.

He reached across the table then, a tattoo of shadows on our skin, and held my bone-swollen wrist in a bracelet of thumb and finger to show me how it was done. My palm was open, wet and afraid; his fingers were light in their circular dance. You have not loved Anna until you've done this, he said. Choreography, free-fall, the passionate forgetfulness. My tendons and soft skin knew and learned and knew.

They'd slept in her apartment. Oval photographs of her daughter stood on the tabletop and windowsill. He had recognized Anna in the rice paper and cloisonné, a hyacinth silhouette. She had mentioned leaving her husband before she turned off the lights as if he were only a word, a fact less than memory, benediction, Amen. Then maintained her height in the sweet cologne dark.

They had slept in his small house. She hadn't seemed weakened by the heat of his cast-iron stove. She'd removed one glove to grasp his hand as they walked toward the pine woods. He couldn't help but talk to her there. His Anna, his only, rare Anna. She'd moved through the snow like a breeze at dusk. He'd fed her soup, kneaded her ivory body, lost himself and gasped the syllables of her name.

You've never seen a woman so alone, he said.

I listened to him and for him. Backward, forward, once again.

You gave her a gift, I said.

I went past what I knew, he said. I wanted us farther in time.

He'd made her a boat—a sub-nosed pram painted like a toy. It had apple-wood knees, a keel of white oak; drawn and cut to last. It was something she could steer, he said. The boat was crazy, extravagant, and she treated it that way. It took river bends like a bowl, buoyant and smooth. She wasn't a woman of the water, but that was his point: she wasn't a kingfisher or a cormorant.

She'd leaned back against the sanded transom, oarlocks empty and flush, her breasts covered by persimmon-colored cloth. Bugs swarmed off the bow. Her long, bare legs were cocked. He tried to describe the dangle of her hand in the current, the pale bloat of refraction, his Anna washed wide. But for once he couldn't speak well enough. Her face was like nothing I've ever seen, he said. There were clear columns of sun from sky to river. The air smelled like hot, green fruit. He had run along the bank as well as he could, but there were gully shadows and tree roots. He had often tripped.

I wanted another glass of wine. That was the way it always was. My long-stemmed glass was blurred and empty; my napkin was like a lotus at its base. He apologized for going on so. You'd think I could speak of something else, he said. It's been long enough. And I would dip my head under his filigree of feelings and tell him no one could cut free fast. He was welcome to go on. I still wanted to hear his voice.

Have you ever been in love like that, he asked. You throw everything overboard, including your oldest ballast; you don't even think about it. It's like your red blood is everywhere, not just in vessels.

In my own way I know what it's like, I said. As if love should be comforted. As if the conduit should ensure an equal, even flow. He rubbed his eyes and checked his denim pocket for a pen. I wanted to show her that she wasn't alone, he said.

Don't you think she was an exotic, I asked. Didn't she glitter a little too harshly?

I see everyone that way, he said. I don't consider it a fault.

Anna had an ideograph of foul summer mud on her cheek when they reloaded the boat that first time. Her nose was pink with burn. She borrowed his rusty blue sweatshirt and she was more beautiful than ever. They'd made love in the truck with the dented doors hinged open, fast and common as children, meshed and carefree, without effort.

She perfumed her hair, I said. She knew how to pose in an embrace. Admit it.

You're right, he said. It was doomed.

You couldn't have believed that, I said. If you did you wouldn't have built the boat, you wouldn't have been patient all those nights. And you wouldn't be telling me this now. The anchor weight of regret is dragging you down. Remember. This is more than failure. This is hope.

You sound Delphic, he said.

Maybe I am.

I'll never forget her, he said. Even her vanishing back was exquisite. Like a dolphin. Or the glimpse of a doe.

He had left his job for a while; he couldn't be there with the algae and the spores. He had built a split-rail fence along the edge of the pine woods instead, swinging his axe, bare-backed.

But he was back at work now, glad he was living simply again. He wrapped a sun-thread curl of hair around one finger.

Was she a prelude to something, I asked. An invocation, a lead?

I've felt that way, he said. She always said I astonished her, yet she left just the same.

The Anna you relive isn't a woman of circles, I said. She eased right past you. She never stopped.

Then I'm the circle, he said.

You're an easy cadence to follow, but it's more than that, I said. You leave yourself wide open. And you expect to hold on to what you have.

You know so much, he said.

I know what I hear, I said. Vespers, whispers, prayers. I've sailed with you over time.

Like a pirate, he said.

Like whatever black flag you want, I said. Every mast tilts at sea. And Anna is gone. She set herself with the first sun in the closest hemisphere. Left me with a spyglass and you with a sextant as you continued to love the cold empty air between points on the map.

You want to see too much, he said.

We swerved with the stars of the zodiac, kept swerving. Do what you like, I said. We'll talk again when the gale behind your eyes blows hard once more, and you see her, or maybe me, with the curved hips of a waterspout in your sleep.

THE GRIEF
IS ALWAYS
FRESH

On the second day of the new year, Marilyn Height's body was found in a frozen cornfield. No snow had fallen since New Year's Eve, and the day had promised to be clear, good for hunting. But the two men from Dixboro were caught short, hunting without dogs along a weed-lined ditch when they saw her. Not that she was hard to see. Her short coat was a pitched dark tent on the knoll. She had fallen after the snow.

The hunters told the deputies exactly what they found—a loose sock in a furrow, some torn cloth on a sharp corn stob. Once they'd seen the face, they didn't touch her, and had to lower their eyes when the coroner found a small pink bra beneath the body, wrapped around one hand. It was terrible, more terrible than either of them could have imagined. She was wearing shoes but no socks. Her small lips were wrinkled and gray.

The sheriff took the hunters' names and addresses, then asked them matter-of-factly how they happened to be there. It was private land, they said, but they were friends of the owner. They watched the sheriff glance over their shoulders as he spoke; the open breadth of the cornfield seemed to distress him. There were only two farmhouses in sight. He'd been searching for the girl for two days, he said, steadily, fruitlessly. Now he had her.

The hunters had left their guns in the truck after calling the police. It didn't seem right to be holding them while they waited in the field, watching the cars and ambulance drive up, broken cornstalks cracking against the silver fenders. But as they stared at the body being bagged and loaded by the paramedics, their hands felt empty and dry. The coroner said she'd been shot from behind several times, small caliber. The hunters had already guessed as much; they took pride in their ability to read signs. The snow on the field was shallow and crusty, but there seemed to be just one set of tracks leading up the knoll. The girl had been on the run. The hunters said they had come out early that morning, earlier than ever, looking for rabbits. They were regulars here. Sure, they read the papers like anyone else. But they never expected to find this, not in a million years.

Sarah had spent the holidays alone, more or less. She had joined the potluck crowd at the Randolph's on Christmas Eve, and Aunt Tottie had invited her over for eggnog, but for the most part, she was enjoying her solo approach to the new year. She'd begin her mornings with a little exploration, setting up her drafting board in a different room each day so she could discover the nuances of her new home while she worked. Parker's absence had left her with a great deal of space. Though she missed her husband in a way she could hardly name, the silence that settled in among the walls as she sketched had become a kind of companionship. Sarah found herself wanting to sleep and awaken with the house—it was a rhythm she found reassuring.

Buying the farm had been her idea. Old farmhouses came up for sale often enough, but she was convinced that this one was rare. The centennial farm—a homestead held by the Schuylers for more than a hundred years—had been listed in the county ads, and Sarah's breathing had deepened when she saw it. She knew Parker wanted to stay in town, near the newspaper, but her enthusiasm had won him over, even when it was softened by the firm pragmatic frown she tried to master for him. She had helped him imagine it—how they'd design a studio for her and an office for him. With patient, thorough care they'd be able to preserve something—not their own history, which Sarah thought of as sweet and sad and unremarkable, but the history of a stubborn, stalwart family of pioneers. That was the beauty and safety of the purchase as Sarah saw it. A restored centennial farm would be a solid but subtle monument, a reminder of human endurance far greater than their own.

The house itself was simple, almost homely. But the repairs it needed were mostly cosmetic; the fieldstone walls and foundations were sturdy. Parker had been so taken with the outbuildings—a large bank barn, a corn crib, silo, and pump house—that he didn't seem to notice the upstairs bedrooms, how one of them was set under the eaves like a miniature nursery. Sarah didn't mention it. It was enough that she could even imagine such a room; it had made her dizzy just to stand there and picture the pastel shades as she listened to the night's

small cries. During one long moment, her stomach had felt like
a liquid dome. And since she couldn't deny the pain of her
miscarriage, she was hoping this house could heal her, this handsome fallow land. She prided herself on her patience, knowing
that if it were steady and rich, the miscarriage would fade like
a cheap, garish curtain in the sun.

She and Parker had told themselves they were buying the
farm on a whim, because it felt right. Parker's commute would
be manageable. And it was reasonably priced, well below temp-
tation. The real-estate agent had tried to flatter them by saying
that consumer demand for the old farms had been low because
it took special people to recognize their potential. But Sarah
knew the truth: rural history did not translate into a good
investment, not in this part of the country. Most of her friends
would never be so impulsive; they'd never buy this sort of house
on that sort of road. Sarah had determined months ago, however,
that her primary concern should be for her happiness, not theirs.
Nothing else, not even the slow, warmly exasperating presence
of Parker was a sure thing. Time gave way, as she knew so
well, to the cost of expectation.

They closed the deal after Thanksgiving.

When Parker told her he'd be gone for three weeks in De-
cember and January, Sarah looked forward to the lack of dis-
turbance. The city was sending a goodwill delegation to Central
America, and the paper had asked him to go along as a special
correspondent. It was quite an honor; they both knew he'd be
crazy to refuse. Sarah smiled, nearly falling over when she stood
on her tiptoes to kiss his neck just below the ear.

"I'll fix up the house so much you won't even know it," she
said. "You'll hardly believe it's yours."

Parker returned her kiss in the solid, attentive manner that
had made their marriage a peaceful exchange for the last three

years. Meanwhile, he couldn't wait to see Nicaragua, to write about revolution firsthand. And she couldn't wait to start stripping the walls.

The first two weeks went well—the weather was cold but Sarah had double-sealed all the windows. She unpacked a few old drafting tools and drew plans for the kitchen, then decided to hang the wallpaper as soon as the ancient gas stove was removed. The floor would be Parker's job.

The dining room and foyer were bare and wood-scuffed, but not in need of much attention, so Sarah spent most of her time in the living room, a jumble of paneling and synthetic carpet that was oddly appealing. It smelled strongly of the previous owners, of pipe smoke and windowless heat. Though she knew the room would smell of her someday, once the carpet was removed and her handwoven rugs were in place, she also knew that the change would be slow and imperceptible, that a house could only absorb what was constant, essential.

It was New Year's Eve and the TV had been on all afternoon. The boys, their uncles and cousins were watching the football games. The floor of the den was already crunchy underfoot with pretzels and chips, and Aunt Paula had made it clear that she wasn't cleaning up after anybody. Uncle Karl laughed and belched. "Happy Fucking New Year," he said, rolling a Stroh's bottle under his heel. "Yes, sir."

Almost the whole Brunansky family was there. Fulton was surprised they all fit into one room. Even without the women— his sister, Nick's sister, Aunt Paula, Uncle Joey's new wife— the den was crowded, though every time Ohio State scored or fucked up, some of them would come in from the living room to watch the replays. His mom spent most of her time walking from the kitchen to the den with plates of sausage balls, staying a minute to steal a drag from somebody's cigarette or to sit on Uncle Joey's lap. It was a loud afternoon, but by the time the sun went down, everyone would be drunk and happy and ready for the parties that night. Then Fulton could get a joint from Tony.

Fulton checked his watch. It was three o'clock, nearly half-time, and his cousins still weren't back. He felt his stomach bend and swim a little. Marilyn had called at eleven; Nick and Tony had left soon after. Lucky bastards, he thought. Tony had pinched Fulton's bicep right to the bone on his way out, cutting a glance toward Nick. "Just a late fucking Christmas present," he said. "Nobody's business."

They had left in the rebuilt Dodge.

Fulton knew why the older boys dumped on him. They didn't have little brothers, and they thought he was a punk, their snot-nosed cousin. But Tony would give him the story later, the way he always did. They'd go to his bedroom for a hit or two and talk about Marilyn or Cindy or the twins from Silver Lake. He'd exhale and tease Fulton with stories broken up by giggles. Then he'd say something like *you'll learn, you'll learn,* as if Fulton didn't know plenty already. When he turned fifteen, Tony said, they'd set him up. A girl with tits like Marilyn. Or the twins.

And yet he couldn't understand why they were missing the Ohio State game. Nick had put on his OSU T-shirt, and had been waiting for the game all morning, saying it would be better than the New Year's bowls because the Buckeyes were kick-ass and fast.

Fulton reckoned that his mom was right. Most guys would do anything for a girl.

The Dodge pulled into the driveway early in the third quarter, OSU with the ball. Uncle Joey knew the boys had been out cruising so he wouldn't let Fulton tell them the score until Nick had brought in some beers.

"Finally got a date?" Joey asked.

"Screw you," Nick said.

Nick hadn't made first string on the varsity football team so he'd quit, saying he might join the army when he graduated, maybe go to OSU after his discharge. Uncle Joey had been in the army, even gone to Vietnam, and had said shit, yes, it was a good place to start, good as any. Keep your head down, ass up, and travel, he said. See the women of the world.

Nick said he liked the sound of that.

Nick was taller than Tony by half a head, and built like the sandy-haired Polack Fulton's mother said he was. Fulton wanted to be like Nick—tall, strong, pure big butt Brunansky, even though his mom said the Amatos, like their son Tony, had been better looking. Tony was his favorite cousin; he was quieter and nicer, Fulton thought, because he didn't have a mom or dad. Aunt Paula and Uncle Karl had moved up from Cleveland two years ago, right after Tony's mother died, and they had taken him in. But Fulton knew that Nick was more likely to play catch or steal a beer for him. He was an asshole, sure. All the guys were assholes sometimes. It was Nick, in fact, who had dumped him off the bunk bed the night before. Mostly, though, Nick was straight and got things done. If you didn't lie to him, he'd treat you fair. Besides, he was one smart asshole, Fulton thought, coming home with a bagful of deli sandwiches in his arms.

Ohio State scored, and the older men headed for the living room, probably to suck their whiskey. Nick and Tony had settled on the floor with foot-long subs in front of them, the wrappers smelling of vinegar. Nick popped two beers, both for himself.

Fulton was reaching for the onion rings when he noticed that Tony was rubbing his hands on his thighs.

"Jesus," Tony said. "Don't you think we ought to wash our hands after that?" His eyes were down, half-covered by dark brown bangs.

Nick didn't answer, just nodded, swallowing noisily. He ran his hands through his hair. Fulton watched them stand up and leave the room, noticing that Tony had a smudge under one eye. Ohio State had broken up a big pass play. Uncle Joey hollered in for the score. The two boys walked down the hallway without pushing or shoving, as if they were tired. Fulton thought of Marilyn and the picture he'd seen in Nick's wallet. *After that.* Tony had told him what *that* smelled like once, a kind of warm and sour stickiness. He felt his stomach fold again. He'd have to get Tony to light up that joint and maybe dig out some magazines too. Shit, the way he saw it, that's what family was for. Especially if you're the little guy.

Brenda Height didn't call anyone until after dark. School was out for the holidays, and Marilyn was free to come and go as she pleased during vacations. But it wasn't like her to be late for a party, and that's where Brenda had promised to take her— to Randy's party. Of course, Marilyn was only sixteen, and who could say what any sassy young girl was really up to?

Brenda called her sister Angela first, but Angela hadn't seen Marilyn all day and neither had her daughter, Carrie. It was Carrie who suggested she sit tight a while longer; some kids had talked about closing down the mall since most New Year's Eve parties didn't start until late.

"I'll call Delong's house," Carrie said. "He might know where she is. He's been after her lately."

Delong? Brenda had never even heard of Delong, but then Marilyn was popular—a different boy on the phone every week. "Would you mind, honey? I'm a little worried."

Brenda showered quickly so she wouldn't miss the phone, then rubbed lotion on her face and legs. But the phone didn't ring. Holding her pink bath towel against her chest, she made a quick call to Julie, Marilyn's best friend, then another to Angela—no news. Her hands shook as she curled her hair the way Randy said he like it. She was nervous about the party. It could be her last chance. Randy would be transferred to the new store soon, and she wanted him to see something special in her tonight.

At nine o'clock, Brenda called Randy to say she and Marilyn would be late because of a mix-up; she was ready to leave except for her lipstick. Randy laughed and told her he'd just tapped a keg for her. "Slap that girl on the ass when she gets home and speed on over here,"he said.

Spotting the half-empty Coke that Marilyn had opened for her breakfast, warm now, and flat, Brenda said, "I will. Don't worry."

The wind picked up an hour later, blowing the morning's snow against the small kitchen window. The wires to the TV antenna were slapping against the trailer's aluminum siding like thin whips. Marilyn's hat and the purple mittens that Brenda had knit for her were lying on the couch next to some fashion magazines. Her note said she'd be back after lunch.

At ten-thirty, Brenda called the police. "I worked a half-day," she said. "Because of the holiday and all. It's not like her to disappear like this. She's a big girl, but she's young." The dispatcher sounded tired and asked if she wanted to report her daughter missing. "Yes," Brenda said, feeling her chest burn under her black lace bra and silver threaded top. "Yes, I do." He told her that they'd have to wait another twelve hours;

juveniles weren't considered missing right away, especially on New Year's Eve. "All right," she answered, pushing the heel of her free hand into the door jamb, thinking of Randy in his straight leg jeans, and Marilyn riding in a car somewhere, laughing with a boy, red-cheeked.

The heat was the most oppressive at night, heavy and breathless. Parker wished he had a different roommate, someone who didn't complain so much and was aware of something more than the dusty wash of the sun—then he might be able to relax. Not that Keppler was such a bad guy, but he was a chain-smoker and seemed to have little sense of anything except the weather and politics. He spent his free time in the plaza, bumming cigarettes and looking for what he called the smoldering firebreaks of revolution.

Keppler was on the city council; he was the reason the delegation was in Nicaragua to deliver medical supplies and goodwill from "the true Americans." A history professor and self-proclaimed loudmouth, Keppler had been happy to room with Parker when the occasion arose. "Glad to keep the press under my wing," Keppler had told him on the bus from Managua. "I'll make sure your eyes are focused."

Sarah would have been a better companion. She would have seen the strange density of the sunset and been able to put it into words. She could have named its bloom and array. Keppler's only concern was the New Year's Day tour; he wanted to see how far the government would go. The government's interpretation of American curiosity had so far inspired consistent but mild doses of forthrightness watered down by a great deal of simplicity. The delegation would be allowed to see a small, neatly dressed military guard at the hydroelectric plant; they would be able to ask the local newspaper editor a handful of pointed questions. But they would be steered clear of the prison and the Cuban-designed civil-defense posts. Developing countries must bare their blemishes modestly. Parker had been told this more than once.

After two weeks of bus and truck rides, fatigue was setting in; even the mayor and hard-pacing Keppler were flagging a bit. There were simply too many affirmations and contradictions to sort out. The hospital had really gotten under his skin. They'd been there earlier that day, in a village near the coast, and he hadn't yet shaken its effect. Sarah would say: *this is the middle ground, this is what both sides share, look hard at this.* And he had.

The doctor had been so tired and beautiful that Parker knew she spoke the truth. Until then he didn't know what it meant to say that someone had skin like copper. She had skin like that, at her temples and the base of her wrists. Her thick, black hair was knotted at her neck. "We do what we can," she said. "I can only hope this next year will be better. I have three full-time nurses and a surgeon who comes from the capital two days a week. I get competent help from the nuns. And prayer. But even with your vitamins and penicillin, there is nothing I can do about the grenades." Her accent was broad, slightly British. She'd been educated in the West Indies. "The grenades are too terrific," she said.

It was the message that Parker had been waiting for, the cool, human plea from the dedicated healer. There were two suspected Contras in the hospital, both young boys who'd been beaten and shot. The doctor cared for them as well as she could. "It is our duty and our sorrow," she told him, intimating that there was no way to make it simpler. "The grief is always fresh."

And in the north, two schoolteachers had been kidnapped by rebels. The marketplaces were colorful, teeming, the tight-skinned tomatoes a testament to the farmers' perseverance, though many of them were women in mourning. The cathedrals were filled; yet the delegation had been allowed to meet with a parish priest only once. The puzzle of this country was unsolvable until you put together the pieces of each and every town. Without Sarah to anchor him to the vigor of the language, the bright and trying landscape, Parker felt that all he could grasp was the obvious truth. *The grief is always fresh.* The doctor had sounded weary but not defeated.

Parker wanted to leave his room for the evening. Their host—an energetic minor bureaucrat—wouldn't mind; he expected the *americanos* to wander. Parker told himself he'd do well to bring in the new year alone, perhaps sit in the plaza and wait for the Spanish bells to ring at midnight. He could pretend that Sarah was with him and that they weren't so visibly alien. They'd see the alleys run yellow with dogs; the breeze would stir the hot village stench. They would wander together past the walled gardens and narrow stucco homes—far from the town hall, away from the Cuban-built housing. And as they walked together, the future would seem to hold itself above the horizon like a blossom in a palm.

Or he could pretend he was somewhere else, not here, in this stale country of death, where new years never seemed to matter.

Sarah's afternoon newspaper was rarely delivered before five o'clock. The price of country living, Parker had said. So she continued to work on the brochure for the spring concert series until five-thirty, when the natural light began to fade. As she washed ink off her hands, she heard the idling motor of the delivery truck at the foot of the driveway. She hadn't spoken to Parker in ten days. She was anxious to read his stories.

On her way to the mailbox in her parka and deerskin gloves, she noticed again how the steep pitch of winter had emptied the yard, how the land was stripped of every subtlety save the muted colors of the season—white on white, gray against brown. She was more attracted to the contours, the way the earth fell away behind the barn, how the house rested so cleanly on the ground beneath it. She liked the promise of the landscape. The snow and the implacability of the ice seemed harsh and barren on days like this.

Parker's byline was on the front page. The article focused on a hospital tour and interviews with Sandinista doctors and health officials. Sarah shared her husband's desire to know what was really going on in Nicaragua, and so she tried to read between the lines, unfolding the paper slowly with her thick gloves as she turned for home. Parker was concise and diplomatic; she knew his dispatches were clearing the censors and editors with ease. Still, she could sense his language growing thinner and thinner. *Ernesto Diaz was wounded in the war. His twelve-year-old eyes are filled with pain.* What kind of pain? The pain of his wound, the pain of fighting his own neighbors? She wanted to know what Parker was burying in that clean sentiment.

She was half-settled on the couch before she saw the sidebar. MISSING GIRL FOUND DEAD NEAR CAUTHEN. She felt her heart lurch a little, then press into a static ache as she continued to read. *Sixteen-Year-Old Shot, Last Seen on Sunday.*

There it was, somebody else's fresh tragedy, the most cruel and useless kind. Sarah leaned back and expelled an audible sigh, feeling the patch and callousness of her thirty-two years. Descriptions of accidents, murders, the ravage of swift disease— she was getting used to them. Parker's months on the local police beat had depressed and numbed them both. Parker had witnessed things no one else wanted to know, things he couldn't even write about. The terrors and losses that his subjects had suffered were sometimes vaguely inexplicable, but they often fit into patterns that seemed destined to occur. The cops, the people at the morgue, everyone whose work was connected to violence and death seemed proudly immune to shock. They'd tried to toughen up Parker. If you want to be revolted, they said, read the papers from Detroit or some of those true crime magazines. Every once in a while we come across something new—like that millworker who cooked his kids in a steel ladle—but never in a town like this. The bad people here may be mean, but at least they're predictable.

Sarah wondered about Marilyn Height, trying to imagine some believable circumstance that would limit the quiet horror of the headline. It was clear that Jack Casey hadn't known much before the paper went to press. There was just a brief statement from the sheriff and a flat "no comment" from the coroner. By now—Sarah checked her watch—he should have the whole story. She wanted to call him, to verify it wasn't a random event, that it had its own logic. Maybe speaking to Jack would lessen the chill in the house.

Cissy, Parker's former intern, answered the desk phone. Sure, Jack was around. He'd been dealing with the sheriff's office all day—it was a total mess.

"Does he have a minute?"

"For you, Sarah, we've always got time." Cissy laughed the loose, raspy laugh of a woman who worked and drank with men. "Talk to your roving husband today?"

"No, maybe tonight."

"Good. Tell him his old desk is trying hard to bump him off the front page." She laughed again. Parker was a soft-spoken, self-contained man. Cissy loved to needle him.

Jack was talking on the line before Sarah had a chance to

say hello. "I knew you'd call." His voice was loud and cocky. It had been six or seven months since she'd seen him, yet here he was, sounding familiar.

"You did?"

"Hell, yes. It happened almost in your own backyard. Cauthen Township. I figured you'd want to get the dirt."

Sarah pressed her spine against the pleated door molding, located the line of her bones. She thought of Parker and more eyes filling with pain.

Jack slowed down, his voice dropping. "The Height killing. That's why you called, right?"

Sarah took a breath. "Yes, I was curious about the details." Her first impulse was to swallow, to say, *I didn't see a thing.* The kitchen windows in front of her were greasy and opaque. Nothing moved in the yard or the fields beyond. She felt her restlessness become a small tremor. "How close?"

"Don't worry. You're nearly a mile away. But the sheriff will probably be out at your place today or tomorrow. He'll just want to know if you saw any vehicles on Sunday."

"Truck or car?"

"Don't know yet. The department hasn't finished the tire casts." Sarah could hear him moving paper around, no longer listening. She heard him draw on a cigarette and imagined his eyes in a hard, creased squint. Jack Casey, the professional. The newsroom was his stage.

"Where was she killed?" She forced out the question, knowing it was wrong to conjure up outlines she'd be apt to shade in later.

"She was found by a couple of hunters in a cornfield on the Reinhart place with seven wounds from a small caliber rifle. It doesn't look like rape, although her clothes were a mess, and she's got no rap sheet. It's not what you'd expect. The mother is a sweet loser, too. But the suspect list is the kicker—a lineup of boyfriends as long as my arm. Not a blessed one over sixteen."

Sarah stared out the window, in the direction Deputy Gage was pointing. "Just about a mile over that way," he said. "Directly northwest." He explained that the girl had been found on the east side of the knoll, twenty yards shy of the fence-line. There was no chance Sarah could have heard it happen.

"A .22 doesn't sound like much, no more than this." Gage snapped his knuckles twice against the door. "Sharp and quick, like a hammer on hardwood."

But the access road was only five hundred yards past her house. She might have seen a truck—they were sure now, it was a truck.

Sarah shook her head slowly and deliberately, as though she were paging through a catalogue of memories. Her silk print scarf slipped behind her ears.

"No," she said, "I'm afraid not." She tried to concentrate, keeping one hand flat on the broad, worn arm of the sofa. On New Year's Eve afternoon she'd been more than a little drunk. The bottle of beaujolais had been empty by three o'clock. The casserole had nearly burned. Parker's promised call had never come through, and she hadn't been a witness to anything.

Deputy Gage and Deputy Heller politely refused her offer of coffee, saying they had several more stops to make. They said good-bye and headed toward the Bass farm next door.

Sarah had promised herself that their visit wouldn't shear off the day, yet she found herself watching the world beyond her house with exhausting attention, as if some giant film reel might screen the ugly sequence once more. The view from the front windows was sunlit. The shadows of fast-moving clouds glided across the cornfields, shading them a deep Russian blue, and easing the sight of the ragged cross-hatching of stalks. She watched the flocking blackbirds rise and fall above the fields, the landscape barely enlivened by their flight. It must have happened in virtual silence, the killer's eyes passing over the frozen spot at his feet. No one had heard Marilyn Height die. The sun had been high but weak. The wind had been gentle but flirtatious—as it can be after a snowfall.

She tried to pinpoint the moment in time when it happened. Between one and three she had eaten oyster dressing directly from the casserole dish. She'd been playing music rather loudly—all four sides of Handel's *Messiah,* some inappropriate Ravel. She'd somehow felt too frail to roast a turkey for herself; a turkey implied guests. Instead she had stretched out on the old green carpet and watched the fire burn. Outside, the skirt of another cold front had billowed by.

Parker had said that she enjoyed punishing herself, that her fears were a form of indulgence. Where had she been when the 737 crashed in Washington or some western river had burst its banks? She always wanted to know. He couldn't imagine why she even considered such things. Yet Sarah believed that lashing her sympathy to tragic scenes she could envision kept her in touch with humanity, the silent, unknown people who were regularly swept away. Exercising her fear prepared her for losses of her own.

She, too, had been rendered forgotten. She had lost a child and would never know if the loss were fate or stupidity. She'd been restless or maybe even careless that day because the child she carried had surprised her. And her own ambivalence, as incipient as it was, had surprised her even more. She had taken a long, hot walk, then stayed up late, very late, inking plates and trying to balance the new print on the press. Neither the doctor nor Parker had blamed her. It happened to many women, and there'd be others, other children. But Sarah didn't think so. There was just one first child; she could be filled, then broken, only once. She could think of no reason why she shouldn't imagine the worst in the years to come. Such thoughts were what she deserved.

Parker was so stable, so solid. He considered himself a purveyor of fact and rationale; his imagination was neither reckless nor macabre. He had seen things he believed most men should never see, things that Sarah could equal only in dreams, and he was seeing them even now. But the sights, their brutality, were so permanent, they gave him a foundation that was larger than life, the only kind he could accept. So he never blamed her for ignoring those first cramps because she was working and time had felt so compressed to her, so hurried and blurred. In some small way, he believed the two of them had been entrusted with memory and the means to preserve it. They—the reporter and the artist—were supposed to feel and respect the truth.

Sarah tilted her head toward her shoulder, pretending she could hear his voice—the thin, gentle voice that made him so easy to underestimate. *A child has died, it happens,* he'd said. *A life is taken and we have to hope for what's given back.*

She rubbed her face with her hands. Her skin felt dry and chapped; her mouth tasted stale. She lifted her coat off its hook and slipped her feet into her cold boots. Keep moving. That was what Parker would suggest.

The snow was six inches deep and seemed to warm the backyard with its reflection. The slanted ruin of the corn crib was chastened by the fresh drifts; even the large hole in its roof had taken on a different shape, the smooth-edged emptiness of a black hole in ice. Since childhood, newly fallen snow, so placid and quiet, had always drawn Sarah outdoors, away from the closeness of bodies and the still, heavy heat of the fireplace. It reminded her of the knowledge that she was forever apart, even in marriage, a blood creature alone.

She hadn't really spent any time outside since New Year's Day. It wasn't the weather that confined her, or even the vague depression she thought she could trace to Parker's absence. Rather, it was the implications of what she considered good discipline, which Parker had once made her confess.

When they had lived in town, she often ventured no farther than her small studio in the garage. Even then she'd resented having to break her isolation—whether it was to buy groceries or deliver a design to a client. Parker had said that she didn't like people, the way they necessarily cluttered her days. Admit it, he said, you're hiding. You turn your back on people because you're afraid.

She had thought that living in the country would be easier. There'd be no one around to avoid. Only acres of free and open land. But now she wasn't so sure; she was already closing herself off—not from people, she didn't even know her neighbors— but from the world beyond her home. The house was becoming familiar, safe. She sensed a clutching reluctance to leave it even for a few hours. What was it Parker had said to her? You have no real roots, you work and live wherever you are. And he said it as though she were being somehow disloyal.

She made herself walk as far as the barn. It was as old as the house, raised by the same family that first cleared the land and plowed it clean. SCHUYLER 1873. The white block letters were clearly drawn on the red siding, right below the eaves. She and Parker had decided to touch up the name and date as soon as spring came.

Once unlatched, the large, square doors rolled easily on their tracks. Like everything else on the farm, they were in good condition. Marge Bass, a Schuyler granddaughter who lived down the road in a modern house, had said that Parker and Sarah could plant corn and probably refurbish the milking parlor if they wanted to; the barn and outbuildings would stand fast for years. "At my place we have three Harvestores now and a brand-new tornado-tough barn," Marge had told them. "This place has finally fallen behind. But I tell my husband every time we drive by that the old homestead is still standing tall, as if it was waiting for something and it's got plenty of time."

The loft had been emptied and swept clean, and when Sarah and Parker had come as prospective buyers, Marge had dared them to find any evidence of rot or decay. Many of the floorboards and ladder rungs had been replaced, and the remaining ones were only slightly warped, worn smooth by years of bales and boot soles. The barn had the original posts and beams; crude hatchet marks were visible along their edges. The permanent smell of cured hay and veils of cobwebs on the beams kept it from seeming deserted. The Schuylers hadn't left any junk behind—no plow blades, no baling wire, no lengths of drainage pipe. They'd truly cleared out, and Marge Bass had been proud of that. "This place was ours for more than a hundred years. I expect we know how to move on."

The ground level of the barn, the section that was built against the slight hillside, had been the stable, then an equipment shed. The stone foundation was whitewashed inside and out, and the latched Dutch doors were crossed in red, a Schuyler trademark. After descending the ladder from the loft, Sarah walked slowly from stall to stall, remembering how she had always wanted a barn as a child, how she'd wanted a place to store her imaginary camels and horses and elephants.

But the earth floor was what interested her the most. Three of the stalls were filled with a dry, flaky soil that recalled the cattle and draft horses that had eaten and slept on it for decades. Even now, the colorless chaff of old straw lay scattered in the corners. The Schuyler children had probably raised ponies or prize calves in these stalls. She and Parker had imagined buying a pony, a tiny spotted Shetland, for their baby's fifth birthday, and all at once she regretted they had given themselves over to such confidence. There hadn't been a pony in this barn for ages, and now she doubted there ever would. At present, just the crusty dirt beneath her feet revealed signs of life. There were rat tunnels in the aisle and under the stall partitions. And, above a slit window, an empty bird's nest seemed to confirm Sarah's sentiment: only the rats remained, clawing and burrowing under the surface. There was nothing in the barn to take with her but the faintly sweet smell of dust.

Sarah found the shells as she was leaving. They were lying loose near the doorsill like a child's marbles or a dozen gold beads without a string. Brass shells. Cartridges. Tilted cups on an upset table. Dropping her gloved hands between her knees, she squatted to touch them, make them real. She knew immediately what they were—an invasion, a cold, plain rupture of the truth, another trespass on the dry, unfertile ground beneath her feet.

Sarah lent Jack Casey a pair of Parker's boots and led him down to the barn on the softly packed trail she'd made the day before. The unpruned apple trees glistened with melting ice that dripped onto their hair and shoulders. She had called Jack about the shells because she didn't want the police to think she was being wildly imaginative. And yet she had to do something. Someone had fired a gun in her barn and she didn't know when. The thought of it made her knees a little weak. She had tried to think through the possibilities. She had even tried to forget about it. Then, as she listened to the orchard thaw, she knew there was almost nothing she could confirm on her own. The Height murder was Jack's story, after all; he had to follow all leads. Before the morning was half gone, she had called him and he'd agreed to come out to the farm right away.

They walked across the frozen ground of the feed pen, approaching the door that was nearest the shells. Stepping through the door frame, she waved her gloved hand toward the hard, pocked dirt before she turned away, leaving him to make his own decision. She had promised herself she would not become morbidly fascinated. Empty bullet casings could have come from anywhere. Unlike the colors of her prints or the intricate reasoning of Parker's prose, most details of the outside world did not connect. It would be unwise to assume that they should.

"Well, they're from a .22 all right." Jack spoke like a man with authority, exhaling as he shifted into a squat. "But they've been here a while. Quite a while, I'd say."

Sarah turned back, pushing the hood of her parka away from her ears. Her lungs tightened as if she were about to cough, and she felt her neck flush, the heat rise beneath her sweater.

Jack gave her his casual smile, rolling three or four of the cartridges around in his palm like small change. "I'm making a guess because these casings are tarnished, too dull to be new. But it wouldn't be a bad idea to tell the sheriff anyway." He stood up and wrapped his free arm around her coat-covered hips, drawing her closer. She stepped down the aisle toward the warped door of the granary.

"Why would anyone fire a gun in here?" She turned to face him. "The ricochet could be deadly."

"Only one reason to go killing in a barn," Jack said, pulling his wool cap over his thin, graying hair. "Rats. You haven't lived here long enough or you would have thought of that yourself."

Back at the house, with their boots drying by the fire, Jack told her that two boys had been brought in for questioning. They were both juveniles. The cops had what they thought was an admissible confession from one of them. But the family hadn't called a lawyer; it might be tough to get the tapes into court. The ballistics report would come back tomorrow—that would make or break the case. The Height girl's best friend claimed that Marilyn thought she was pregnant by one of the boys and she was frantic for money.

"Oh God, you mean they shot her because they thought she was pregnant?" Sarah's throat went dry.

"They started out trying to scare her, I think. One of them, the Brunansky kid, said a baby would—get this—ruin his life."

Sarah felt a new uneasiness slipping into her. *A ruined life.* It was a singular, desperate idea that could take shape more than once in a lifetime. Her drawings, her plans for motherhood, her marriage—much of what she had once desired could now be identified as rubble, though as a heap it was still habitable; some lighter part of her continued to live in its midst.

"They shot a girl to save themselves from a baby?" Her lips tightened.

Jack reached for his cigarettes. His gray eyes narrowed as he lowered his eyebrows, a look Sarah had seen before. "I'm sorry."

For a moment, he was silent, smoking his cigarette while she closed her eyes and let the tears come. She'd always found it difficult to grieve alone; now that someone was with her, she could allow herself to unravel. She heard him push his chair back from the table. "I'm sorry," he said. "I've upset you and you're alone out here. I forgot what you've been through."

She didn't see him move toward her. The flood of old desire was loosed by the weight of his hands on her shoulders; her eyes were unable to telegraph restraint. The contact felt strange and acute within the shell of her sorrow. Those hands were his signature, so reflective of Jack, so insistent and probing. They were her greatest memory of their few months together, so different from her own, almost hesitant, hands.

"Parker is a shit for leaving you now. This political stuff is scraping him hollow."

"Don't bring him into it," she said. "I'm okay."

"You're not okay." His hands kneaded her neck, slowly but firmly. "This place is like a tomb."

She opened her eyes. The kitchen counters tilted and faded. This was how their affair had begun all those years ago. She had collapsed in his direction, rewarding his persistence with a moody dinner date that led to four months of pensive, irresponsible passion. She dropped her chin to her chest, feeling his fingers work themselves into her hair, telling herself that she shouldn't be thinking about the past or the future, that she couldn't afford it.

"Do you trust me?"

She nodded slightly, her lips pressed together like her eyelids.

"I'd like to think we've always understood each other." He dropped his hands back onto her shoulders, then lower, running his palms across her breasts.

Sarah didn't love Jack, and she loved intrigue even less. All she asked was that he stay with her awhile. It was a matter of taking what was given without forethought or retreat and making use of it.

She was the sort of woman he feared, he said, because she was so hard to ignore, a woman who knew how to use a man's own code of behavior against him, but he followed her upstairs anyway, flinging his newly lit cigarette into the fireplace and holding her hand when she offered it.

He was silent while they undressed, unlike the past, when it could be said of Jack Casey that he talked his women into bed. Sarah wondered if it was the burden of Parker's presence that made him quiet, and she found herself taking stock of her husband's possessions. There were a few books on his dresser, a tangled rack of ties on the wall, and a small portrait—one she had drawn not long after she met him—hanging above the wardrobe like a mask. But it was true that Jack had never liked Parker much, a fact he had made very clear when Sarah announced their engagement. So it was hard to believe he might be squeamish.

And yet her own confidence was not an easy posture to maintain, even after Jack drew her into his arms and began to stroke her hips. The room was brightened by the diffuse light of an overcast sky. Jack's body was shorter and thicker than Parker's, and Sarah sensed that the veil of memory that had swathed her so warmly at first was beginning to tear. She felt an arousal that was more irritation than bliss, but she made a choice, however small and mean, as the slung curve of Jack's belly overtook her. She wasn't going to struggle.

Closing her eyes in a haze of comfort, she didn't think of Marilyn Height or her shadow child or the hands that must have held the gun. All she felt was a heartbeat pressed against her thigh; she heard nothing but breath. Jack always made her feel mortal: full and flawed and bound by certain limits. Parker had let her lapse into his idea of perfection, as if she were amorphous and sweet, barely able to be held.

The funeral was Friday morning and most of the relatives left town that afternoon. Filling the sink with hot water so she could wash the percolator and a stack of pie tins, Angela begged

Brenda to stay with her through the weekend. But Brenda said that she had to get back. Both sisters were drawn and red-eyed because they hadn't slept, and Angela's turquoise kitchen was choked with hours of cigarette smoke. Still, Brenda couldn't miss the hard cut glance of her sister's eyes. "I know what you think," she said, her voice thin and sore. "You think I've got nothing to go back to."

There wasn't any way to explain herself now, even though the two of them had buried their mother four years earlier and had spent hours together then, talking their way through their childhood. This time Angela hadn't been much help. The minister hadn't either, although Brenda was sure he'd be at her door the next day. Only the coroner gave her something she needed. He had shown her the body with the straight, clasped mouth, the hair pushed back all wrong, and said, *There must have been a mistake. Your daughter was never pregnant.*

She promised Angela that she'd call if she began to feel sick or depressed. But she had to go home on her own, she said. Marilyn was still with her in a way she couldn't express, and she wanted to be near that presence, which was no more than a shimmer and a shape behind her burning eyelids.

She ran from her car to the icy cold door of the trailer as fast as she could. Dropping her purse on the sloppy rectangle of three-color carpet, Brenda wished once more that Albert had been able to come up for the funeral. She'd practically thrown the damp receiver into her sister's hands after she'd tried to talk him off that Texas oil rig, breathing hard while the memories slid through her mind with the clear focus of photographs. He'd cussed over the whine of machinery and said he'd try to get away. For her. For his angel-haired Marilyn. After all, they had once been a family.

But he hadn't made it.

Brenda couldn't sit in the living room. The idea of watching TV seemed plain crazy, and staring at the worn couch littered with mittens and gloves proved to her that Angela was right—even the silence was alive. Angela had made her swear to keep away from the closets and dresser drawers; you should never rush a clearing-out because it couldn't be done, she'd said. Marilyn's clothes should remain where they were for now. The door to the small bedroom should stay shut even though the bed was unmade and the air smelled of Marilyn's perfume. Only Brenda's bedroom was empty enough for her to bear. Except for Marilyn's eighth-grade picture, which was taped to the wall, the room was all hers. But even there, Brenda was tense and nervous and thought she heard sounds, as if her body were coiled and waiting for the front door to fly open under a restless hand, then slam.

She decided to take a ride, a long one. Maybe she could somehow clear the road behind her. *Be back after lunch.* Marilyn had taken care of herself the way Brenda had always told her she should, screamed at her a million times, in fact, in the years after Albert had left.

Keep your ass out of trouble, young lady. I ain't rich enough to bail you out.

Brenda backed the Nova onto the pavement and headed south. The weather was warmer now, just as it had been at the cemetery. The snow on the windshield and mirrors had melted; she could see exactly where she was going.

She'd had so little to tell the police. Marilyn's friend Julie had pointed to the Brunansky boy and his cousin, saying how Marilyn had thought she was pregnant and wanted money to get things straight. Julie had been at the church service, near the front, but she hadn't said much to Brenda except that she was sorry, so sorry she could hardly speak. Brenda didn't have any words for her either, so she simply asked Julie to take one of the pink chrysanthemums from the lid of the casket, just take it.

The whisper of regret, like the hot edge of an approaching headache or the swish of balding tires, got louder as Brenda drove. Everybody had said it. *Those boys are crazy, sick, they ought to be shot, put away.* Only the minister had refrained. He said he felt the sweet hand of God.

Brenda turned right after the Trenton railroad crossing. *Will of the Lord.* She'd been driving almost by instinct, paying no attention to road signs, but when she crossed the icy rails of the poorly kept tracks, she suddenly knew where she was: Cauthen Road junction.

Brenda parked the car next to an aluminum gate and got out, her eyes strained from tears and lack of sleep. *Somewhere in a cornfield.* The gray and white folds of land fell away in all four directions, like an old moth-eaten tablecloth. Between two farmhouses, one made of stone, the other framed by blue silos, lay acres and acres of soil in narrow, frozen pleats. A beige pickup with a dog in the back sped past her, spraying her legs with slush.

She walked to the chain-latched gate and pulled herself over the top with a speed that matched the pace of her heartbreak. She would find it; she would find the place of dread. But as she turned her head from side to side, searching for a landmark, she knew she was lost. The fields, the sunlit gates, the stand of black, leafless trees gave her no clue. She had thought she would know the spot on sight, know the way a mother can identify her daughter's nighttime cries. But every field and hedge seemed frightening and possible; every fallen branch, every leaning fence looked like a sprawled and broken child. And there was no trail for her to follow. She pushed a fist into her mouth and bit hard to keep her stomach down. Her hands were numb and bloodless. She couldn't begin to think the words, though she knew them now, she knew the worst. Her little girl had died in a place that had betrayed her with cold indifference, a landscape that only changed with the drift of the seasons, and she hadn't left a mark.

Detective Grusak waved at the two-way mirror; he began again. Tony's eyes burned; he wanted to talk to his aunt one more time, to make sure she understood that he wasn't responsible. But he knew better than to ask for any more favors. Grusak was pissed off.

They had been shut in together for more than two hours. The room was a lot like interrogation rooms on TV, Tony thought, except that TV had overlooked a few things—the way the creamy yellow walls got closer when Grusak was sitting in front of him, for example. When the detective pulled at his tie and circled the table, sometimes stopping behind him, Tony felt less crowded. It was easier to slip down in the dark metal chair and relax.

There'd been a long discussion with Aunt Paula before the questions started. She didn't want him to hide behind a lawyer. Tony was to tell what he knew. He wasn't so nervous now, not like he'd been when the police had come to the house and Aunt Paula had slapped his face. He had told them he had nothing to say, and she'd reached up and hit him twice across the mouth. "That girl is dead, and you knew her," she said, her lips shaking but her eyes set hard. "Now tell your story." She had pleaded with him to tell the truth. "It will be better for your soul," she said. "We have Nicky to think of, and the whole family's heart is broken. Imagine your mother's eyes in heaven and speak true."

Tony knew they had tape recorders on the other side of the window. He just wished Grusak and his partner, Minton, would lighten up. They kept asking him the same questions over and over. Why did you kill Marilyn Height? Why did you take off her clothes? He said as little as possible, but that didn't stop them. They simply rewound their questions along with their tapes.

"Okay, Tony, let's start at the beginning." Grusak turned away to tuck his shirt into his pants. "How long was Marilyn your girlfriend?"

"Never. I already told you."

"You stole her from Nick," Grusak said, tossing a pencil onto the table. "Come on."

"I didn't steal her. I never said that." His face was beginning to sweat again. They were trying to mind-fuck him. "We were just together sometimes."

"Together?" Grusak bent over his chair, his brown necktie swinging. "You mean you slept with her?"

"Maybe."

"You shared her with your cousin Nick?"

Tony could taste the sour metallic tabletop on his fingertips. He pushed his hands into his lap.

"You picked her up on Sunday."

"We saw her around."

"You picked her up in Nick's truck, took her to Cauthen Road, and shot her with *your* gun."

"No way." Tony needed some fresh air and the chance to take a piss. The little room smelled like fat Grusak. "You know it's not my Goddamn gun. My aunt told you." Tony felt his voice getting high and drawing him out of his seat as if a string were being yanked through his throat.

Grusak stared and waited for him to sit back down. Then he leaned forward, his breath bitter with coffee. "Your cousin tells me different."

So that was the deal, Tony thought. Use Nick to set him up.

After he'd gone along to keep Marilyn cool, convince her to be quiet. He figured they'd done enough by freezing her ass and scaring the hell out of her. Nick had wanted her to take care of the abortion herself, and not tell anyone. Tony knew it would be the last time they'd see her, but he could live with that. Seeing her pasty white face puffy with tears, having her kick him hard in the balls had cured him of ever wanting her again.

"You know it's not my gun," he repeated. "Uncle Karl bought it for Nick before I ever lived with them."

"But you're the one who shot it." Grusak looked like he was trying not to smirk.

Suddenly, Tony was crying. Too hot, too mad, too exhausted to hold it back any longer. He choked a little before saying, "You fucking do *not* know that. That's a lie. A Goddamn lie. I didn't shoot anybody, I didn't mean nothing. All I did was scare her." He felt the thud of his fist against his thigh; it was far away, dull. "Just scare her."

The detective pulled a handkerchief from his pocket and handed it to Tony. It smelled of mint cologne, like something Uncle Joey might slap on his face before mass. "Just *scare* her?" Grusak's eyes were bloodshot, nearly expressionless. Tony realized that the guy reminded him of his old little-league coach— tough, distant, taking him right to the edge. "Tell me about Nick and Marilyn," Grusak said for the third time, raising his hand toward the large silver mirror again, his fingers straight. "Tell me now how it went."

Parker called just before midnight, but the connection was weak and fragmented. Sarah heard the quick melody of the operator's Spanish behind each of his fading sentences. He was at the UPI office in Managua.

He wanted to know how she was, sounding almost casual, a habit he had of locating himself. Parker had a private use for every routine. And while he talked about the travel delays and Keppler's indefatigable lack of organization, she found herself becoming impatient. Just tell me you'll be here, that you love me, and hang up, she thought. But she knew that she had fallen in a deep pool of escape, and listening to Parker's slow, groggy voice, she knew that he, too, was hanging from some sort of ledge.

She'd been waiting to hear from him since dinner. Jack had called to tell her about the delegation's delay; he'd been kind but brisk. He wouldn't interfere. In return, Sarah promised no encumbrance. The hour, the event did not haunt her, not yet; she was trying to close her mind to it.

Parker's words hummed across the distance—high then low, staccato then slurred, suggesting a fatigue that was more than dislocation. He wasn't wavering in suspicion; a man like Parker didn't waver. He didn't even speculate, not about his wife or his home. This was Parker grieving for himself, deflating in a country of poverty and strife, and Sarah could hear it. Her husband was leaking. He was draining away.

"Parker," she said. "Are you all right? Are you sick?"

He hesitated a moment. "I'm just worn-out, I guess."

He was barely audible, his words a used thread of his own weaving. She realized she was rubbing her thumb along the edge of the kitchen table, something she did when she was preoccupied. She was almost amused when he asked about the house.

She ought to tell him the truth, she thought; their home was gray and unflinching.

"I'm trying to take charge," she said.

"I love you," he said suddenly. "Work hard. Draw something for me, okay?"

"I love you, too," she said, imagining the bright arc of their conversation, its nearly impossible reach.

He hung up first, and she listened to the connection try to end, the receiver clicking and snapping as satellites made their intention a minor impulse. She and Parker were separated, and it occurred to her, as it often did, especially when she was working her inks or her printing plates, that they really didn't know each other. She had prodded, second-guessed him, left him happily alone, and he still hadn't opened up to her. She felt the weight of their failure fall through her chest. She could try again to give him a child. But that might cause more apprehension and fear. What would it give either of them but a second chance to die?

Nick hadn't thought about hell since he was a little boy, and he probably hadn't thought about it then. His mom and the priests he'd grown up with in Cleveland were the only people he knew who seemed to take hell seriously. Hell, purgatory, fire of eternity—it had been a lot of talk and worry; it didn't have any real effect on the world. And when you grew up the way he had, swearing that you'd never end up in a steel mill, wanting the car and clothes and job you deserved, the real world was all that counted.

And yet there was this feeling in his stomach, a sort of nervous flame that he couldn't shake. It began when the cops brought him in, and now, on the skinny bunk in the detention center, it was still with him. It didn't matter if he were wide awake or trying to sleep, he felt its constant nagging. He told himself to ignore it and not to give in to anything. It all came down to knowing he was a man.

His mom had said it was his hard devil soul that had taken him away from the Merciful Lord who would forgive him if he would repent; his dad had to hold her back for everybody's good. But she whispered and yelled anyway, saying what were you doing, what have you done to us all?

He didn't know. It had been so easy, like slicing a page clean from a book. He could remember it, sure, though the details were fuzzy. There hadn't been a decision, just one long held breath and the slightest sensation of cracks in his bones. No shouting, no anger, no hesitation. A reflex maybe. A rock striking home.

The cops and the doctors were trying to drag him through it, trying to get him to put a bunch of words to each shot. But they were wrong. They wanted him to pay for it, and they were wrong. He had felt almost nothing, and that was all he'd admit. The strange white shape of Tony's face, the long sucking spasms, came later. Then the nagging pilot flame.

A man could do almost anything in a moment. He could fuck little Marilyn Height in her doorway. He could fire a gun. The stories you told eventually wore themselves out until the real way you'd moved and thought was lost forever, even to you. A man was never direct. If that were so, he'd probably still be out there, shifting and tight, capable of sticking to a promise and a threat, full of quiet, rushing blood. Instead, he was here where it was hot and dull, where they'd make him remember their outrage, make him imagine a made-up pain and confess to a mouthful of thick, sloppy lies.

She stood at the bedroom window trying to gauge the passage of time by the slow rotation of the blue-shadowed moon. There was a moment when Sarah wanted to believe that the biting wind was sweeping the sky clean; she wanted to feel that wind on her skin, in her home. But airing her brittle memory wouldn't change what had happened. The betrayal would be there—not as a scar, but as the shiny, hard surface of her heart.

The fact was unforgettable, and though she vowed to live past it, to treat the man and the afternoon as a single gesture, half-formed and fluid, she could already feel herself wavering.

Parker was coming home. Flesh would soon meet fatigue— the peculiar alchemy of reunited love that she wasn't sure she could bear. He would see that she hadn't gotten along well without him, not even for three weeks; she was pale, thin, a little frantic in her touch. He would try to comfort her.

It was the bleak image of Parker's forbearance that finally drove Sarah out of the house. She hiked across the snow-covered yard toward a collage of shadows on the road, plunging into snow that was up to her knees, leaving a rough trail behind her.

Once she was beyond the house the air seemed lighter, more pure. She lifted her arms out to the side as she balanced on a beam of darkness. The wind wrapped her skin in a necklace of cold.

As she walked toward the fields, she told herself that it was a pilgrimage, a sacred search for some source of courage. She wanted to forget her own history; she wanted to escape the gnarled nest of her own mistakes. Naked beech and maple trees creaked and swayed above her, abandoned by the night. When Sarah craned her neck to look at their thrashing branches, she was chilled by the strength she saw rooted in their bend and obliviousness. They were so much more beautiful and less dangerous than she, because they used their power to protect themselves. They could only be ruined by others.

So she started to run, run toward the same frozen ground on which Marilyn Height had died—imagining her tearstained face, the shocked pivot of narrow shoulders, the feet that seemed to move too slowly.

As she turned onto the unpaved road, she ran faster, and felt cool rivulets of sweat down her back, heard the rasp of her own breathing. There was nothing left of her homebound body that she wanted to reclaim. The snow gripped her knees with its stubborn, crusted drifts, and she drove her legs like the torque-worn parts of a threshing machine. She moved as if the killer were right behind her, the light weight of a rifle seesawing in his hand. He was slow and deliberate. She had time, the earth curved; the land tilted toward the horizon. She turned her head, twisting to see over her aching shoulder. He'd have to sight and reconcile; he'd have to find her in the shades of dark beyond him. By then she would be on the crest of the hill and in flight.

She tripped on a cornstalk. Robbed of her agility by a new exhaustion, Sarah tumbled and rolled. Her collapse was nothing like death; there was no turning toward sound or light; her head wasn't washed clean by bells. She scraped down the icy bank, covered her face with her hands and drew her bruised knees to her chest.

She landed in the groove of a ditch. The loose wires of a fence were just above her. In daylight she knew that the limber stalks of sumac were ripe with oxblood shoots, and the thin bark would show teethmarks of animals. But now the wild fringe of field was a black tangle.

She stood and felt a movement in the darkness near her feet. Startled, she took a half-step backward, and saw a fist of shadow shoot up toward her face. The cry caught in her throat, harsh and primitive. She was still choking on the sound when the rustle of feathers began to fade.

Sarah felt her chest loosen. She must have broken into a roost, a bird's home. She backed away as carefully as she could, wiping her nose with a trembling hand. And as she stepped onto the white clarity of open snow, she knew that this was where Marilyn

Height had been killed. A dark cradle in the earth was behind her, the snow was broken on the hill, and she knew. The deputy had described it like this—as desolate as a storm-washed sky. She might have expected a column of haunted air to mark the spot, but Sarah felt more than the ghostly absence of death. Marilyn Height hadn't been able to outrun the rifle; her fear couldn't be imagined, even as punishment. What Sarah had brought upon herself wasn't tragedy. She was a weak woman. Her scars and flaws wouldn't end her life. Whatever she had lost—and maybe it was too much—she had simply, foolishly, given away.

Sarah turned toward the knoll, then turned again. The soles of her boots swept through the snow until she was spinning slowly, the moon the only spot unwhirled. If she kept her eyes open, she thought she could clear a space in that timeworn earth. She would have to dig. She would be frail, and that would be the only word for it, scraping through the cold crust to find the fertile loam below.

NATIVE
REST

I hold a letter from my brother Matthew in my hands. His handwriting is large and upright, and he signs with his initial, a stiff-legged M. Written in blue ink on his white business stationery for Piedmont Feed Supply, it says that he's sold the house and all the land, even the pine forest that Jack Cannaday stripped and ruined ten years ago. Our mother has moved into the small, carpeted apartment attached to his kitchen. As we agreed, she'll receive the tiny profit from the sale.

His letter is succinct. I'd like to think that being succinct means he's comfortable and contained in resignation, but it doesn't. My brother has truer, if harsher, instincts. He knows exactly what has been lost. The farm is gone, and I am living way out in Tidewater, practicing medicine in a town that is sinking in the marshes between a naval air station and the Chesapeake Bay. I don't have any right to complain, to speak and make the words hang on, and everybody knows it.

If I could tell them the story of my growing up and turning away—the slow, frightened moment I set myself in retreat— I'd want it to sound as true and clear as the call of a cardinal on a lone cedar branch. But it wouldn't. It's a terrible thing to be always falling back like I am. A terrible, tangled thing. I just didn't want to fail; I didn't want to be tied to a ramshackle homestead the way my father was. I thought I saw beyond it. I wish I could see my brother scratching his short, dusty hair under his Piedmont cap, scratching and nodding while he said *Things change, everything comes and goes.* And yet I can barely envision him in my mind's eye when I stand on my new redwood deck smelling the moist rise of the tide.

I think about our neighbors, the Old German Baptists who farmed right down the road. They wanted to be overlooked and timeless. They never dwelled on weakness, not the weakness of one person or his entire family history. When I was a boy and the lives around me seemed lost and indirect, my neighbors treated their weaknesses as if they were hard bones. At least, that's the story I tell myself—the story of what I didn't have and never wanted.

Mrs. Bowman is folded in her wheelchair. The house is quiet, nearly empty, because it is well past noon. Her sons and her black-hatted husband are in the fields to the north, cutting silage. She can hear the whir of the blades, the high buzz of the drive shaft. Every few minutes a son—Jacob, Emory, or Lap—guides an overloaded truck past the house toward the silos. The gears twist and grind under their impatient hands. She listens to their mistakes.

The kitchen is warm and smells of kale, sweet potatoes, and brown seed rolls. She kneads the dough, seasoned the old way, at a child-height table near the stove. Norah has prepared the rest. A tiny, quiet fifteen-year-old who looks like a Schultz, her mother's people, Norah is a gracefully efficient child. With her wheat-colored hair and wide-set eyes, she could be from Indiana, she could be cutting ginger snaps while the wind swayed ragged millet in the fields. Instead, she is in town with Rachel Boone, buying small-print fabric, keeping her eyes to herself.

The pain in Mrs. Bowman's legs is infrequent now. It has been two years, and although she thinks of her legs as dead, she allows Norah to wash and dress them every morning. The disease is sorrow to her neighbors, a trial for her husband. But Mrs. Bowman does not allow the grief to waste her time. She kneads dough, sews when she can, and maintains a becoming silence. When her sons carry her up the spoon-gray steps into church, she grasps the corners of her black crocheted shawl and nods to the deacons with open-faced humility.

She wants very little before she dies. Perhaps a larger freezer. Perhaps a heavy, accepting embrace from her husband, Isaac. Though these desires are the only worldy wants she has for herself, she can be at peace without them. What she must have, however, lest she stumble at last in despair, is the assurance of her sons. She wants to see them into manhood—witness their marriages, their housewarmings, the purchase of their tractors and herds. If she can watch them settle around the vale of their parents' home, sharing land and equipment and labor, if they will wheel her toward the foundations of their dairies, her chair pressing its tracks into their yards, she will be done. She will end her longing for the hot, hazy wind of Indiana, for the fine hem of its dust.

Mrs. Bowman tilts her head forward until the edge of her white prayer cap brushes her shoulder. Her neck is aching. With the thick smell of pan grease in her nostrils, she listens as a wavering yowl rises above the windowsills.

It's the cat—the thin, pregnant calico which has left the empty dairy in search of food. She will have her litter soon. And Lap, Mrs. Bowman's youngest son, will have to drown the kittens. He will take them across the bull pen to the river. He will carry the burlap sack, tied shut with twine, close to his chest until he reaches the weed-choked bank. He will add stones, and close his eyes. With his arms straight but shaking, he will heave it forth, knowing that his father and brothers have given him little time, knowing that his mother is watching.

When we first moved to the country, my father often told a story about the farmer who once owned our land—McCrory, MacDonald, MacLeish, no one remembered the name exactly—how he stood on the hill above the house and played "Amazing Grace," over and over, on bagpipes. One tune, heirloom bagpipes, two feet planted. No kilt or foolishness. Just a wail that pierced the air and ran the farmer's eyes with tears. Some folks laughed, but most didn't, not after they stopped along the road at sunset and heard the deep gasp of that hymn. It wasn't like the gut-humming of a banjo, which went right to your bosom. The pipes had a certain historic quality. And you couldn't deny an old man that, the way you couldn't deny our neighbors their privacy.

The Bowmans, the Altices, the Boones—we would do well to leave them be, my father said. They dealt only in cash, and dealt well. Sure, they were strict and more pious than he'd ever be, but the Bowmans had been able to lease three of our fields when our steers were sold at a loss, and the Altices were happy to lend us their baler. Working for Mr. Bowman wouldn't be too bad, he said. When he had the loan to buy new calves and repair the pens, Matthew and I could have our old jobs back, working for him. In the meantime, we were to learn what we could. The final fact of the matter, my father said, was that we all plowed the same sweet dirt.

Norah's baptism is her favorite dream. Mrs. Bowman contemplates her sons all day long, but when she sleeps, however fitfully, it is her daughter, Norah, who fills her mind.

For the baptism, Norah is very tall, much taller than she is in real life. Trim and demure in white, Norah's skirt billows like a storm-filled curtain as the elders lead her to the river; her pale, strong legs are smooth, hairless. Her hair, though it is pinned and braided by custom, is subject to change. Leaf brown, rust brown, corn-syrup gold—in the dream, it is likely to be any color except the color it really is, which is what Mrs. Bowman remembers when she wakes. A true baptism would never be like this.

At the ford, the chief elder blesses Norah in a soft, urgent voice. His bleached shirtfront and squarely trimmed beard echo the stark profile of the church, just a few paces away, up the slope. Mrs. Bowman has to shade her eyes from the smoke-yellow sun. She can't guide her wheelchair too close to the river because the water is magnetic, the water draws; it could pull her in. While she narrows her eyes, brow sweating beneath her starched cap, Mrs. Bowman feels an ancient tingling in her knees. Only the chief elder and Norah remain at the ford. The rest of the congregation unfurls upstream like a banner. The wind smells like stone.

The chief elder reads from a Bible no larger than his hand, his dark pants rippling about his thighs. Norah is beautifully obedient. She blends herself gracefully with the deep, moss-tinted current that is suddenly broader than Mrs. Bowman has ever seen it. The elder's pressing hand is a blurred shape on top of the girl's head. The submersion is swift. If the dream continues, Norah will rise crisp and dry, bound to God and a husband who is sometimes the sturdy, heat-baked elder, sometimes a stranger at the corner of Mrs. Bowman's eye. More than anything else, it is Norah's moon-round face that is so wholly bewitching to her mother—the frail woman who dreams her. It remains unchanged by either water or touch.

The dream makes her restless. Thankfully, it usually comes right before dawn. Once awake, Mrs. Bowman tries to lie still next to her bulky Isaac until it's time for him to rise and tend to milking. She straightens her arid bones as much as she can, remembering the verses her mother always read to her, in a voice that dangled from the faint rhythm of a German accent. Through half-open windows the morning air smells of burst grain, dew, and manure. The cows gather and low. Blessed are those who hunger, my child, blessed are those who thirst.

It was the summer our farm had failed, the summer I turned fourteen. I was late for work at the Bowman's one afternoon, riding my bicycle toward the good farms, the homes of the Old Germans. When I reached the gravel crossroads, I slowed down, then stopped. The barbed-wire fences on both sides of the road were upright, newly strung and stapled. I could see the Holsteins in the barnyards, patient and swollen with milk. The sun lay a halo over the high tassels of corn. The houses were white, the sheds were white, and the dusty gravel under my tires had been pressed into waves by thick tractor tread. I heard the bark of one dog, the shout of one child near the river. My breath panted in my ears.

The radio wired to my handlebars was playing loudly, and I turned it off, the way I always did when I got to the top of the hill. The Bowmans didn't believe in radios; I'd promised my father that I wouldn't use mine. Matthew was in bed with the chicken pox, so I was facing a day of silence, a day where I would have to fill troughs and scrub teats twice as fast. My head would begin to bow, my arms would shake. The Bowman sons wouldn't laugh with me unless the cows stomped on my feet.

That's when I decided to go home, through the brown and gray shadows of dusk. The handles of my bike grew cold underneath my sweaty palms. As I passed the tangled honeysuckle along the road, I remembered my brother's eyes pale with fever. My father had said it was possible for me to do the work of two or three boys if I had the determination. Instead, I found myself pedaling past the driveways and cattle grates, looking for a mark in the mica-flecked clay, a place where the earth or the air above it changed. My stomach felt dense and smooth. Where did our bad luck end, I wondered. Where did my home begin?

My parents' house sat in a steep valley above a muddy creek. The porch was peeling; the tenant cottage didn't have windows or doors. We didn't have a real barn anymore, just a backless aluminum shed and a rusty diesel pump. My mother once said that the whole farm looked like a rustic painting, no matter what time of day or season. And she was right. The twin mimosas, the tapered boxwood, the puzzle of handmade brick and mortar—they held the valley light as if they'd been arranged that way in a lovely, waning portrait of the land. And yet, all I can picture is the day I quit for good.

Isaac is beating Emory on the porch. This should not be difficult for Mrs. Bowman to bear. She understands discipline. Discipline rests firmly in the palm of the Lord. This is Emory, however, not Lap. This is her sixteen-year-old son, and the arrhythmic sounds of his punishment are thudding against her heart.

Her dark-browed Emory is as tall as Isaac, his deep chin is shadowed with stubble, and his mother often thinks that he will be the first to marry. Fraying the seams of his britches and shirts, he exasperates his sister, who must constantly alter his clothes. Though Jacob will inherit the homeplace, Emory might be considered the better match because of his empathy and charm. Yet he is weak, perhaps untrustworthy. A gate has been left open, and the new tractor—a full-throated Massey-Ferguson—is in a ditch. Mrs. Bowman understands the unspoken words that Norah and Jacob have strung tight between them. Emory oversleeps, he is red-eyed. He has been sneaking out at night.

Mrs. Bowman rolls her light and silent chair down the hallway. The crack of Isaac's belt is heavy in the hazy summer air. Isaac can be cruel when unfettered, and he has never had to beat a son so old. He will be unforgiving. He will swing until his lungs wheeze and his eyes are rimmed with sweat because he needs his strength for nothing else. Tonight, all the chores will be Emory's.

Mrs. Bowman wishes the beating was in the barn, or the feed shed. But Isaac will not strike his bedeviled sons in a place where he might be seen. He has hired extra hands for the summer, neighbors who are sons of the doctor, and he does not want to fail before them. They expect a lot of him because he provides so much—piety, serenity, frugality. His fields are lush and well tended; his herd is fat.

Mrs. Bowman doubts that Emory will cry. He is stubborn—the broad-shouldered, slate-eyed son of his father. He bathes in his pride. Still, she listens. For he has the throaty, feathered voice of a Schultz man, best given to the rich tonguing of German. When he speaks, he lifts her memories on his lips. When he sings, scooping a hymn from his chest to the sweet instrument of his mouth, he is a minister, a maker and healer, a trumpet of God.

She doesn't think it would be possible for him to give tune to pain.

Mrs. Bowman would like to reforge him. She cannot abide his failures, even though they are small flaws in an otherwise perfect vessel. She wants Emory to be firm; he is her continuity and gift. Above hull and rind, he must flourish. The full branch must bend only with time.

I played a trick on the Bowmans after I quit. I filled their mailbox with M-80s and blew it loose at the seams. I imagine they knew who had done it. Two days later a new mailbox appeared—simple, aluminum, screwed to a peeled wooden post. On Saturday, when Mr. Bowman arrived to count his dry heifers, the ones grazing our fields, he paid my salary to my father from a wide scroll of bills he fished out of the zip pocket in his overalls.

The next week my brother and I announced to the rest of our neighbors that we were available to load and stack hay until the end of summer—twenty dollars a day, lunch included. The market for beef cattle slid, then crashed, and yet my father maintained his optimism. He said that he was lucky to live in such a fertile part of the world. Sometimes, on his afternoon off, he'd ride the hay wagon with us, no matter who we were working for—the Altices, Wheelers, or Furrows. He'd talk to the other farmers—German Baptist or not—about the weather, slaughterhouse prices, even church. Most of them had been his patients at one time or another. Occasionally, he'd step into a kitchen to check someone's pulse or swollen goiter while we swung our hot legs from the porch.

The truth is, much of what I recall about those years are glimpses and nods that didn't belong to me. I wanted to keep my past quiet and dim, settled in a way that reflected the mortal ambitions of my parents. My father tried to be a farmer for four years, raising polled Herefords and surplus hay. When he failed, he had to reopen his clinic in town. Matthew and I never got our hand-raised calves to the state fair, we never drove a new model tractor. And yet my parents remained in the old house as the front porch sank and sumac crowded the fence-lines and creek. My father stayed until he, and all possibility, died. He mowed the fields they had leased out, grew beans and tomatoes for my mother to freeze. He often talked about what he might do later, and for him, talk was enough.

Jacob and the veterinarian are cutting calves. Isaac wants to raise at least four steers this winter, and, according to him, they might as well be his own. The rest will go to market when they are healed and the price is right.

Mrs. Bowman can see the cattle chute from the pantry window. Lap's bobbing head, and red billed cap, becomes intermittently visible as he drives the frightened, splay-legged calves toward the headlock that Jacob draws shut. Lap's whoops and shouts are vigorous and playful. He has fed these little bulls every day of their lives; they know him well.

The veterinarian stands opposite Jacob, shoulders hunched. He wears large green coveralls that are stained with manure and blood, especially below the waist. His rubber boots are splattered with mud, some of it fresh. As he speaks to Jacob, he places a new cigarette between his lips. Jacob appears not to notice, though Mrs. Bowman knows that her son is always aware of fellow men.

A black-faced calf is caught in the lock, and begins to bellow. Mrs. Bowman reaches forward to rub a smeared windowpane with her shawl. Her breath mists the glass before she cleans. She wishes Norah would not be so careless.

The veterinarian and Jacob make quick work of it. Mrs. Bowman cannot see the dark eyes roll or the fleshy nostrils flare, but she can tell when the cut is done. The calf is quiet, and the veterinarian slides back between the wide, gray boards of the chute, his pale gloves glistening. He drops the hanging flesh into a bucket, leaving Jacob to wash and daub the wound one last time. The cigarette wags between his lips. Squinting even in the shade, he grinds it into the trampled soil.

Before the calf is released, he is given a shot of medicine to prevent infection. Mrs. Bowman nods as she watches the veterinarian fill a large syringe with fluid. It is similar to what her neighbor doctor still does for her, slow-beat ritual, followed by a well-practiced sting. As Lap steps near, brother shows brother how to tap the vein. Facing the sun, the veterinarian empties air from his needle, holding it upright and clean like a candle. Jacob moves away, rubbing his straight-line bangs with a forearm. In front of him, Lap peers over the calf's neck, cotton tufting from his fingers as he swabs its skin.

They castrate six calves in two hours, changing the animals' lives in one bright stroke. Mrs. Bowman knows that only the bodies are affected—the length of back, for instance, or the breadth of neck. Cattle have no other history, she thinks. Their first loss, their mother, is their final one.

Before the veterinarian leaves, Jacob comes to the house for his gift. Mrs. Bowman has tapped her stiff fingers on most of the jars in the pantry. She has decided on relish, the sour kind. The jars are arranged in a shallow box; each lid is covered with a clean gingham cloth. Jacob smiles at his mother, his shirt striped with filth, his chestnut hair plastered in waves. She nods, then frowns at his boots, which are brown and caked. He apologizes, but Mrs. Bowman remains stern. She believes Jacob must know continuous disappointment, even in the cast of his dutiful smile.

The veterinarian is embarrassed by the gift that Jacob tells him is for his wife. Still, he accepts it with a handshake. Mrs. Bowman knows that his wife has just borne another child, a boy, and that Isaac has called this man many times in the night. And he will be summoned again—when a calf is born breech, when a virus spreads. He belongs to no church. His sand-colored hair is unruly, badly cut. His college, she remembers, was Georgia or Tennessee, places where she has no family. But he is kind and young and necessary. Her sons cannot be veterinarians. Her sons must be schooled in other ways.

I returned home a few times after the fields had run to thistle and my mother had given in to the sag of the house. Now a paint salesman will try to live there. He'll try to bring up his children and their ponies past the weeds. He'll be the one to hack at the honeysuckle and chase the wandering steers off the road.

The last time I went back was in late summer, when the

neighbors' rye was a blinding green and the ribbons of their fields followed contours only a close tread could know. The home I had tried to forget was gently framed in the unfailing light of August. The eastern knoll was like a bread loaf, the slow stream like a crease. I heard a flock of starlings spatter the withered apple trees in the steep valley, silent for nothing, never still. I felt how they too had bones hollow for flight, blood thin for leaving.

My mother shed a few tears that evening as we drank iced tea with mint on the porch. We watched the sun burn into the smooth brow of Orchard Mountain, and she said she didn't regret a thing. I reached for her hand, which was as dry as a husk, and kept myself perfectly quiet, my feet absorbing the endless cold of the fieldstone steps, my heartbeat muffled.

Isaac has taken her to bed. This is usually Norah's task, though Mrs. Bowman does what she can to ease the burden. She washes herself in a tin basin and loosens her own slack clothing. She can do everything, really, but pull herself onto the mattress. The bed is high and old-style. It was her mother's.

Tonight, however, Isaac has sent Norah to her room. They will have guests tomorrow, distant cousins from Ohio, and the girl needs to rest. Mrs. Bowman feels the tremor of her husband's concern as she undoes her hair. She braids alone while he bathes. Dropping each slender pin into a pine box carved by Emory, Mrs. Bowman listens to the whisper of her settling family. Trickle of water, slide of sock on wood. She strains to hear the creak of secrets. Nothing. The children bow and pray like crocuses. Isaac lifts himself from the tub in a rush of water.

Mrs. Bowman knots her long, ash-streaked hair. Her gown, shapeless and unadorned, is over her shoulders. It will take Isaac only a few patient tugs to free her skirt from the cold weight of her thighs. She wraps herself in a lap rug, gasping when her husband touches her with a wet hand.

Bare-chested, he carries her as if she were fragile, a child. The laugh she spills is like a sneeze, it comes so fast. Glancing at her, Isaac furrows his brow, and she sees the yellowed, failing picket of his teeth. They have known each other for more than thirty years. There is nothing that cannot be explained.

He dresses himself in the far corner of the room. His breath is even, the fabric of his skin is like linen. If he plans to speak, he will do it now, before he opens the Bible. Between cicada and dawn, this time is theirs. Otherwise he will only bless her, and thank the Lord for her strength.

He asks first about Norah. Then Jacob. The cousins from Ohio have two sons, one with his own dairy. There will be questions, and Norah may be invited to return the visit, perhaps for a whole summer. They also have two daughters, twins the age of Jacob. The cousins are known to be less traditional; just the oldest son has joined the church. Isaac wonders if his wife is ready for this, if she can think of sparing Norah for so long.

Mrs. Bowman believes that Isaac can never understand her readiness. He is an outward man, a man with few reserves. But Norah is too young. Perhaps another year, after the church conference. Her relatives will be here then. And the Old German families from California. They should all bide their time.

And pray, Isaac says. Mrs. Bowman assents. She reaches toward the end of the bed, her thin hand no more substantial than a doll's. Isaac's wide, hard palm clasps hers. There have been nights when such communion led to kisses, to clamber, and weight. But that is dusk memory. She has borne the children. The seed has root.

Mrs. Bowman lies back as Isaac opens to the chapters of

Exodus. He will read aloud until she sleeps. With her eyes closed, the light waves across her lids like fronds. Isaac's voice is the shot, uneven patter of rain. With the tail of her braid against her cheek, Mrs. Bowman parts her lips with a heavy tongue. She has lived here all her woman's life, in a fold of clay and air. There is blood in her temples, heat in her wrists. The refrain held in her throat is like a harrow on a hill, a rattling sift. Once a girl, a smock, a field elsewhere—she has claimed this earth with spine, now native rest.

KETTLE
OF HAWKS

At a certain place, during a certain time of the year, hawks gather to fly together. Once joined, they wing so thick and deep they appear scooped whole from the white loam of sky. Before long they separate, diving to spend the rest of the year alone or in pairs, scattering like ash or well-cut paper. They are uncanny and habitual. They forge their "kettle" with relentless instinct, then break it with cool, swift skill.

I

He didn't smell like anyone Abraham had ever known. Alfalfa, cold water, and the dry powder of oats rose from Tom's jeans whenever he loaded hay or rehung a paddock gate. Abe would remember the distinct, sometimes sour air that surrounded Tom well into the night. Although he expected Tom to be different—he had studied history at the university and came from a city family—Abe didn't believe that Tom's past could account for his scent. Tom had been living in a barn and managing mares too long for his background to be anything but flat, broken detail. Abe trusted his instinct because it was part of him, like the quickness of his hands. He knew his mother was unbreakable; she held things to herself. But Tom Price was a mix he didn't understand.

Abe's mother, Miriam, knew how he wanted to be out of the house, away from the low tin roof and warped sills that were all they could afford. She'd encouraged him to get a job at

Vintage Ridge and to work hard for Tom, learn what he could. His father had worked for the Cabells—mowing fields, painting fences, and tending foals—before he joined the army. After his father was killed in Vietnam, Abe and his mother stayed in North Carolina for sixteen years. They had come back to the valley along the Ragged Mountains because his mother had always believed there was a place for them there. She had grown up and first fought for herself in one of the tenant cottages tucked on the Ridge. And though she never talked about it, Abe knew she remembered what it was like to win the long quarrel that had made her a little bit more than Michael Keenan's wife. He also knew that she wanted him to square off like that now, while she was still there to show him how. Mrs. Cabell, school, the demands of Tom Price would be challenges, extra weights on his back, but he would bear them. He was all Keenan, with the stone-blue eyes of his mother, the last promise of his parents' life together. He wouldn't falter.

Abe loved working on the farm. He and Tom would feed, clean, and turn out ten mares by the time the school bus stopped at the gates of Vintage Ridge. Even in the lonely dark of winter, before the first swallows skimmed the fields in silence, Abe wanted to move through the sunrise. He was seventeen and felt strong; taller than Tom Price, he was able to stack a hayloft on his own. He wanted to be hot with sweat when he walked into the classroom. It set him apart. Some of the boys in his class worked, too. The Halifax brothers milked fifty Holsteins twice a day. But Abe was working the best land in this finger of the Shenandoah. The Cabells had brood mares, a stud, and two back pastures running with Black Angus. Already he had learned to guard what he had—closely and carefully—as if the burdens of someone else's farm might actually be a gift.

Abe didn't spend much time with people—really no one other than his mother and Tom. Elleck McGee managed the Cabells' holdings west of Ivy Creek, so he was around sometimes. As were a few girls—the ones who pestered him for help with their math—but they were for the summer, Abe believed, when he'd have some evenings free, and the fields and horses could grow lush and fat on their own. Until then, Abe stayed where his mother could watch him from the fallow cornfield below their house and see his red jacket fade in the dusk that settled behind the barns.

Tom worked Abe hard—that was his reputation. He needed one man to help him bring Mrs. Cabell's breeding operation into rhythm, a man who was strong, quick, and intelligent. Tom Price knew his business, and whoever worked with him, worked to learn. Abe halter-broke weanlings; he checked foals in utero and memorized each mare's cycle. Tom pushed him, it seemed, not to break his spirit but to keep his own self intact, separate— the most complete self that could be made from soil and season and the mute trust of animals. If he had a life beyond the four-board fences of Vintage Ridge, Abe didn't know about it. Tom was one of the best horsemen in the county. He exacted his wages and the respect of everyone who knew him. He didn't seem to need anything else.

When Abe applied for the job, he knew he was only one name on a list: he was young, ignorant of the subtleties of breeding, probably eager to a fault. Tom had hired him anyway, mostly to please Mrs. Cabell, who'd seen Abe's father work his way into the army. She told Abe she had a weakness for the handsome Keenans. But he could tell that Tom Price didn't do many people favors. There was a hard, glinting look in his eyes when they shook hands—as if he wanted to let his new employee know that he had every right to ignore and disrespect him.

"You think you can handle it, Keenan? You like horses?" Tom had just finished giving him a tour of the barns.

"Yes, sir. I'll do my best."

"Your best?"

"I learn fast."

"Yes, well, Mrs. Cabell has already told me what your best is. She says you've got a nice ass. Like your daddy." Tom gave him a faded gaze, hard to read. Maybe humorless, maybe tired. Abe thought he'd be lucky to last a week.

Once he was on the job, Tom was polite, though distant. The bruising order of work didn't blunt Abe's curiosity, however. While they shared the chores, Abe found himself amazed as Tom's walk, his expressions, and even his smell belied his reputation and all the rumors of the hell he could raise in one glance. Yet Abe kept searching for the flaws he'd come to acknowledge as the price of age and experience—and couldn't find them. Few wrinkles, no scars, no handicaps. The face, closed and quiet as it was, didn't look any older than his mother's. Thirty-three or four, he guessed—a little younger than his father would have been.

In truth, Tom's whole demeanor seemed whittled down, squeezed into the precise life of a manager. Abe wasn't sure why he thought there was something odd about that—he and Tom didn't talk about anything but work. Still, he considered Tom a puzzle, and he would think about him at night, after his mother had closed her bedroom door to be alone with a magazine or the books that were so plain in her hands. Tom Price wasn't that different from his mother, Abe thought; they both craved their silent routines, the sameness of the weather and the hills. They both kept their lives very small. In fact, there was an aspect to his mother's restraint that bothered Abe. Not that he felt she would hold him back—he could pretty much do as he pleased. He didn't suppose his mother would deny him anything, though she would shield him, first on one side, then the other—just so her life wouldn't change. She was only acting

to protect herself, he guessed, knowing she might never blossom
again.

Abe thought it was arrogant of Tom to be so alone. He knew
that people pulled back from the face of death. But no one had
the right to play their life as if it were always on the keel of
tragedy, apt to lean into the hard waves of pain at any moment.
Abe didn't think that was fair. He had survived poverty and
the early, haunting loss of his father. Tom Price, after all, had
come from somewhere—a home with money, he imagined, and
perhaps a long history. Even Mrs. Cabell treated him, her mud-
stained employee, as an equal. So what had Tom Price lost that
made him so remote?

If it weren't for his hard-edged honesty or the way his hand
would shade his deep-set eyes when he gazed into the sky, Abe
knew that he would have quit long ago. He couldn't work for
a man made of nothing but cold bone. A man like that could
drag a boy down. And yet, something greater than Tom and
his curious ways was keeping Abe there.

Sometimes he thought it was the horses; he and Tom were
good with them. Sometimes he thought it was the roll of the
land, how he was able, on some days, to pretend Vintage Ridge
belonged to him. Often, however, he'd just shrug it off as an
instinct, a trying patience inherited from his mother, an understanding he knew would unknot itself in its own sweet time.

One Saturday morning he was left to bathe Ragged Time,
Mrs. Cabell's young stud, by himself. The order was tacked to
the bulletin board in Tom's office. *Wash R.T. first.* Abe had
never been asked to handle Ragged Time alone—the horse was
powerful and full of himself—and to bathe him before he'd
been fed, when he was sure to be restless and defiant, was unusual
and difficult. Still, Abe would do as he was told. Not because
he wasn't wary and didn't have a mind of his own, but because

he thought, as he always did, that he could succeed. Tom Price be damned.

Abe clipped the chain-link end of the lead line across the bridge of Ragged Time's nose; he would need it for discipline. Watching out for R.T.'s teeth, he removed the stable blanket and led him toward the washing stall. The barn was quiet except for the skitter of a few sparrows down the aisle. The mares were in the brood-mare barn across the main paddock, so R.T. was likely to behave if nothing distracted him. With R.T. in crossties, Abe hoped he'd be able to bathe him, rub him dry, and walk him out before too much of the morning was gone. If things got rough, he could always twitch him; he just needed to work fast and keep R.T. as warm as he could.

Ragged Time walked onto the concrete floor of the washing stall, head down. He seemed a little sleepy, as though he might not mind a good rubdown. Yet Abe knew better than to relax. R.T. was not like the mares or Kimbel, Mrs. Cabell's hunter. R.T. had really never been broken. He was a stud, a beautiful physical specimen with the temperament of a bad and jealous boy. Elleck wouldn't go near him and even Mrs. Cabell handled him only when Tom was around. But Tom had disappeared, gone to the main house for coffee or to check the back pastures, leaving Abe with the challenge of a little dirty work.

He removed the leg bandages that R.T. wore when he was in his stall. Then, reassuring the animal with a hand along his hindquarters, he slipped into the aisle to fill a bucket with warm water. R.T. fidgeted, loosening his stiff joints and snatching at the crossties that swung on either side of his head. When Abe moved back along his flank with a full bucket and sponge, Ragged Time stomped a well-shod hoof on the concrete. He was hungry and impatient.

"Hold on, you son of a bitch," Abe whispered, running his

palm along the crest of R.T.'s neck. "Just hold on, and we'll
have you fat and happy in no time."

He started just behind the horse's ear, soaking the wide muscles of the neck and shoulder with water. R.T.'s coat was short,
and his thin skin was laced with a hot network of veins. Abe
could smell the muskiness of the stallion's flesh; the broad back
quivered as water trickled down the curve of the ribs. He dipped
the sponge into the frothy bucket and squeezed it between his
hands. His own veins stood out like rope. He drove his hand
between R.T.'s front legs and scrubbed.

He was working his way down Ragged Time's belly when
he heard the first nicker from the paddock. The morning had
grown warmer, and the sunlight seemed to carry the sound. A
nicker, then a playful snort, told him the mares were loose.

Like Abe, Ragged Time didn't need to see them or hear the
light pop of their hooves on the frost-hardened ground. The
mares were there, closer than they should have been, and so
R.T. began calling to them, his chest heaving, the muscles in
his back flexing tight as a fist.

Abe tried to calm him, but it was all he could do to prevent
him from rearing right out of the stall. His only option was to
hang onto the lead line while the chain dug into the tender
bridge of the animal's nose. Since the wet concrete floor didn't
offer much traction, Abe was sure that the horse would be under
control in a minute or two. If he could close the aisle doors,
then R.T. could raise as much hell with the crossties and barn
walls as he wanted—just as long as he didn't get to those mares.

When Abe tried to move past, Ragged Time flattened his
ears and swung his quarters, trapping Abe before lashing out
with a front hoof. He missed, but his intention was clear. Abe
lowered his shoulder and shoved hard in return, staying close
to R.T.'s chest so that any more kicks would be useless. The

tangy musk filled Abe's nose again, and he could feel R.T. drop his head and reach for the exposed muscle of his shoulder. "God damn you," Abe shouted, yanking hard on the lead line, his hands aching. "Don't get fucking mad at me." The startled horse stopped for a minute, his head high again, his nostrils flaring. Abe thought he had his chance. He'd go out the small door that led to the front of the stall and secure the barn before the damned horse had enough time to hurt himself. Letting go of the lead, he shoved R.T. once more to distract him, then backed off toward the door behind him.

But he wasn't fast enough. Ragged Time caught him below the breastbone, and Abe fell back, feeling like a hot pipe was piercing his lung. Hooves and the small eyes of an animal gone wild with desire flickered above him. He willed himself to fall toward the door. Through the sudden dimness of his brain, he wanted more than anything to be out in the air where his throat might at least open in a cry. He stumbled first against wood, then against something less firm, collapsing and hoping he was safe.

It was a moment before Abe realized that he could lower the shielding forearm from his face and try, really try, to breathe. Tasting the iron tang of blood, he felt himself gulp like a child, his arms limp and afraid to touch the burning center of his chest. He drew himself into a ball, tears in his eyes, and waited. It was the only way he knew how to survive: wait, you will feel better, though not much better, in time. Tom Price had pulled him to safety, but he was gone again. There were hints of cursing and scuffling in the dull, washed ringing of Abe's ears—Tom might be tending to R.T.—and Abe sensed he was back on his own. One minute. He'd get up. Wipe his face and nose. Beat the living devil out of that horse.

Tom reappeared in the doorway and helped Abe off the hard

ground, supporting him with an arm across his back. A few mares crowded the board fence behind them, tossing and anxious for the sound and scent of Ragged Time.

"I'll need to take a look at you and listen to you breathe. Make sure the lung's not punctured," Tom said. "Looks like a mean blow."

Abe nodded, one hand moving tentatively over his ribs. "I'm all right," he said. "Just give me some time."

"No." Tom was firm, demanding. "I have to take a look."

Abe tried not to flinch when Tom sat him on a bench in his office and unbuttoned the work shirt that was wet with water and soap. The large tanned fingers were cold, flat, and slow-moving. Abe shivered, and Tom withdrew his hands, rubbing them for a second on the back on his jeans. "Sorry. Got to do it." Then he started again, following the arches of bone across the curved abrasion that was already becoming a bruise. "Tell me if it's real bad anywhere," Tom said, his voice even and unconcerned. "If it stabs."

Abe gritted his teeth and watched Tom's mouth and jawline. They composed the face of a warden, someone who maintained a sturdy order. All this while Abe's skin and bone hurt like hell. He thought if it wasn't for Tom's hands—the careful, knowing way they probed his pain—he wouldn't be able to stand it: the distance, the nonchalance. "Relax," Tom said, going over the core of the bruise once more. "Try to breathe easy." And Abe tried, his hand gripping the sanded edge of the bench, his eyes rimmed with tears. He watched the top of Tom's head, listened for sounds beyond the barn—anything to keep himself from shaking.

"Well, I don't think he even broke a rib, not badly anyway." Tom stood up, the smell of worn leather and mud rising around him. "I'll get you some ice and take you home."

Abe rubbed his face with a dirty sleeve. The skin over his throat and collarbone tingled. "Bastard of a horse," he said.

"Hey." Tom took a step backward and grabbed his work gloves from his pocket. "Don't blame R.T. Not in my barn. You're the smart animal around here."

"I didn't let those mares out." Abe tried to stand up without doubling over. He wanted to leave. His head hurt, his nose was running, and he was damn close to crying, something he'd never do in front of Tom Price. "He trapped me."

Tom reached for Abe's collar and pulled him straight up, his face still with tension, his eyes flat and nearly yellow. When he whispered, the words came from the back of his throat. "Blame nobody but yourself. You want to be a man around here, you take care of yourself."

Abe didn't hesitate. "I always have," he said.

"Fine," Tom said, turning away and putting on his gloves. "The ice is upstairs."

Abe was able to limp across the office and take his jacket from the coatrack, but he could tell, in those few steps, that he wouldn't be able to get himself home. He'd have to call his mother, meet her at the gates. God damn, he wanted to walk out of there unhurt and unmarked. He wanted to prove to Tom Price just how able he was. But he could hardly move; his whole body was aching, growing stiff. Leaning against Tom's desk, he tried again to catch his breath. He could hear Tom moving around in Ragged Time's stall. The man's voice was slow and gentle, a murmur above the soft wood and shavings that absorbed so much of the barn's sound. He was calming the stallion, taking care of him. Abe rubbed his pounding forehead. Tom had a way with animals, but with people he was empty and slack.

Abe made his way down the main aisle with his shoulders

square, his hands by his side. He muffled occasional coughs with his jacket sleeve, not allowing himself to think about the taste that was at the back of his tongue. He would walk home if it killed him. He was well past Ragged Time's stall before Tom stopped him. "You're never going to make it. Do you have to be a damn proud Keenan about everything?" Abe turned because he wanted to hit him, to crack Tom Price with something real across the face. He was close enough for a good, quick punch. But Abe couldn't raise his fist, even when he thought his body would give him that much strength. Tom was too near, his hazel eyes opening dark, almost warm in the shadows of the roof beams. With one move, a hand to Abe's shoulder, Tom made himself into another man.

"You need ice on those ribs and a place to lie down," he said. "Let's go upstairs."

Tom lived above the office in a private apartment that Abe had never visited. He had to brace himself against Tom to make it up the stairs although he felt, with each step, that Tom could have lifted and carried him whenever he liked. Once inside, he wasn't very surprised. The space was neat and sparsely decorated. It was dryer and sweeter than the barn, filled with air that was close but not dusty. Tom sat him on a single bed that was covered with dark wool blankets. A bookcase and lamp stood nearby. While he took off his jacket and opened his shirt, Abe scanned the walls and the sharp pitch of the ceiling. Almost empty. A few pictures of birds and mountains. No photos, no human faces anywhere. The only decoration that he recognized was the darting song of the swallows that came from the one small window and from beneath the eaves.

Tom had him lie back, bare-chested, on the bed. Then he pressed against Abe's ribs one more time. "It's sometimes easier to find a break when you're lying down," he said, his fingers easing the dull pain that radiated from the bruise that had risen like a dark moon. For a moment, Abe shivered beneath the touch. Tom was like a doctor, only worse, because they weren't in an office; they were on the wrong sort of ground, in a place where it wasn't easy to give in to pain. But the slow fingertips continued to generate warmth through his body, leading him toward the crest of sleep. As he drifted, he felt the pulse of his skin against the pad of Tom's palm. He barely moved when Tom lay a cloth-wrapped bag of ice on his ribs.

Abe pressed his head into Tom's flat pillow as the ice began to sheathe his skin with cold. Lying with his eyes closed and tired, he listened to Tom sift through a dresser drawer and thought of what his mother would do for him when he got home. Rub his temples, maybe. Fix him a bath. "My Ma will come and get me," he said, trying to keep his voice steady. "She won't mind."

"Okay," Tom said. "I'll give her a call. Put this on so you won't look too worse for wear." He laid one of his clean, dry shirts beside Abe. "We don't want to worry her."

Abe sat up, ice sliding over his bare stomach and leaking onto the bed. He reached for the shirt, realizing his ears were still ringing, not knowing for sure whether Tom was speaking to him in a whisper or not. He saw that Tom was also undressing, changing his work shirt for something lighter and fresher. He was across the room, his jeans low on his hips, his back brown and hard in the filtered light. Even with his face hidden, Tom appeared at ease, almost familiar. Abe was a little embarrassed. Somewhere in his stomach he felt as though they both ought to be moving beyond the dull, lazy recovery that seemed to follow accidents and linger in their wake. Otherwise, he thought, something would shift, and he and Tom would never be the same. They'd be ruined by favor and change. That wasn't what Abe wanted; he wanted a chance to meet Tom halfway. Rubbing his eyes as if to widen them, Abe sat up, leaving the ice to drop in a puddle on the floor.

Abe buttoned the shirt in silence, noticing with a smile that the sleeves were too short. Tom was standing near his small refrigerator, not speaking or letting Abe know what he owed him for this sort of kindness. Abe could only stand so much quiet. He examined the bookcase and the floor around the bed. Wildlife encyclopedias, books about plants, histories—Abe didn't recognize any of the titles. There were some feathers, a whole group of them, laid across the top of Tom's books the way Abe spread keys or change across his dresser. "Hey, Tom," he said, reaching to touch one. "Is this from around here?" The feather was crisp, almost brittle. "I've never seen one."

After a second of silence, Abe thought maybe Tom was laughing at him. There was something quivering in the air—unspoken, barely heard. But as he turned to face Tom, whose shirt was open over his solid chest, he couldn't be sure what it was that he saw beyond Tom's expression. He only knew that he felt as if Tom had crossed the room to stand beside him, even though the man hadn't moved.

"It's from a red-tail hawk," Tom said. "The rest are from other birds, hawks and buzzards mostly. One is from an eagle."

Abe looked at the long, graceful feathers. They were large but delicate in silhouette. He stroked a light-colored one with a finger. "You like birds?" he asked.

Tom was quiet again. His face took on the single, flat shade of morning light. "I flew birds once," he said, releasing his breath. "A while ago. I kept the feathers for repairs."

"Repairs?" Abe felt Tom's footsteps, the pine floor creaking.

"A man can fix a bird's wing or tail if he needs to. If he knows how. I used to do it some." He stopped in the middle of the room, and Abe felt his face flush as the words came on, easy and slow, like the breeze from Tom's walk. "I flew a lot of birds," he said. "I could whistle them out of the sky." He dropped his voice and glanced over his shoulder toward the glaring alcove window. "But that was many years ago. When I was young and wanted to do perfect things."

Abe's throat tightened. Tom was blinding himself with the white sun, freezing in a swirl of harsh dust and light, and Abe realized they had come too close to something that mattered, to some failure or story he didn't want to know. Then Tom lifted a hand to his face and stepped backward, and the exact square of sunlight was empty.

II

Miriam didn't allow herself to be shocked. Certainly not in front of Abe, or in the face of any fact. When Tom Price called from the Ridge to ask if she could retrieve her son—that was the word he used, *retrieve*—she spoke one word into the receiver and hung up without allowing her speech to bloom into expectation or worry. Abe wasn't dead. When that happened, Miriam knew she would feel the sear of absence long before it took on the hard shape of notification. Her son was alive, alive for pain or disgrace or discharge, none of which could take him very far from her. After Michael's death, she feared only one thing— the distance of abandonment that finally, after shallow days and months, made memory a relief. Michael had been dead the day his company left for Vietnam, but he didn't stay dead—not in her heart, her eyes, or the deep center of her body—until she met the casket in Delaware on an afternoon so hot that flags hung like wet paper and the brass of the military band sounded like an innocent whine.

Abe, though, was alive. Each time he came home to her, he stepped from shadow to precious child. When she watched the heft of his arms and caught the rhythmic press of his feet, he was a truth she didn't have to caress to believe in.

Miriam took off her apron and pulled her hair back with a rubber band before she lifted the keys to the truck from their hook. She'd been cleaning a chicken when Tom called, and her hands smelled raw and cool, as if they had been digging in the morning frost. She wiped them on her thighs—a gesture that mother and son shared—and left the house without locking the doors or turning off the radio that was filling the kitchen with melody. Miriam didn't prepare against intrusion. She believed that whatever wanted her or her home would be stealthy and thorough despite any effort at closing up and shutting out. When time, the dilapidation of change, knocked against her, she tried only to recognize its beauty. She told herself she trusted its strength.

So Miriam didn't hurry. As she drove down the driveway and along the creek, the grind of the pickup's small engine flushed dove and cardinal and lark from the brush. Miriam watched the birds that so gracefully scattered in fear. They didn't seem to err, even in desperation. They possessed great skill on the wing, she thought, skill their predators must envy. Turning through the lattice gateway of Vintage Ridge and bearing right, she parked as close to the main barn as she could.

She had already climbed out of the truck, the cloud of its exhaust still billowing above the ground, when she saw Abe open the aisle doors and begin to walk toward her. He smiled as if he were okay, but the weak swing of his right arm and the imbalance of his careful steps echoed an injury. Her son was by himself, empty-handed, the muddy dangle of a shirt flung over one shoulder. He waved to her not to come closer, not to block his path with any sort of concern. She understood him—hurt and stooped as he was—and got back into the truck. Her son spoke the unspoken well. She didn't look at him; instead she kept her gaze fixed on the worn paddocks and fields of the farm. The land was cold, still, and bare. There was a flash of color along the back fence, and Miriam knew that Tom Price was watching. Her son continued to walk toward her in a wide curve made to accommodate the drawn hunch of a bruised body against the apparent emptiness.

When he hoisted himself into the truck, Miriam didn't ask any questions. Like his father, Abraham had always been able to articulate his needs—few and disparate as they were. She would take him home and go on with her morning chores until he asked something of her, asked politely for a bandage or a ride to the clinic in Ivy. Then they would draw together into that brief, tight fist of mother and child. She might touch him, he might ask to rest against her arm for a moment, and their grip would be single until time brushed them back into the separation that made the plain daily sadness somehow easier to bear.

They didn't talk. Abe supported himself against the dashboard while Miriam steered the truck past the creek, the white sun in the corner of her eye, the whir of frightened, soft-breasted doves just beyond the windshield.

Her son managed to reach the kitchen table before he asked for help. "I think," he said, smothering a dry cough with his sleeve, "that I need some more ice for my ribs."

Miriam nodded as she retied her apron. She tried to seem only slightly curious.

"I got kicked," Abe told her, propping himself against a chair, "and I need a bath, too."

Miriam watched him limp into his bedroom, his jacket falling from his shoulders. He was too proud to tell her the story, to talk about whether he'd been stupid or not. He always kept his mistakes to himself, just as she did, and hid his little victories too, most of them, letting them trail behind him where they could never quite catch up and assure him that everything was fine. He was quiet that way, but Miriam was sure his silence was mostly for her sake. He knew joy and enthusiasm; she thought he could recognize real passion. But he was restrained with her because he knew that she had willingly taken to living her life beyond commotion. And he wanted to be kind.

Taking an ice pack and a towel into Abe's bedroom, she knocked on the bathroom door before she entered. The water was running fast and loud, but Miriam could hear her son above the flow. His voice was strong but coarse, as if the words were catching in his throat. "Come in," he said. "I'm in the tub."

Abe didn't care when or how his mother saw him naked. Modesty was not a thing between them. Miriam walked in and stood over the tight, bare body that was being washed with waves of clear hot water. Abe lay back, his eyes closed; the clench of his fingers on the edge of the porcelain tub was the only sign of pain. The bruise that Miriam saw below his breast was purple and swollen; it seemed to be bleeding under the flesh toward his hip. It looked like a scythe to her, a blackened scythe moving to cut, and she couldn't help but feel its hurt and ugliness. Bending down, she placed the ice on Abe's breastbone, letting him grasp the pack and move it onto the bruise. He gasped, and his blue eyes opened, gazing into her own. "Cold," he said, smiling through his wince. "Going to be all right though. Tom says nothing's broken."

"Is Tom a doctor?" she asked, thinking a wound like that must mean something was cracked or shattered.

"No, but he checked." Abe relaxed again, his left hand floating wide and free above his thigh. Miriam was always surprised to see how beautiful, how like his father he was: white and solid and muscular, completely opaque and whole even under the broken light of the water. His legs were long, too long for the tub really, and they were covered with the same thick, soft hair that Michael used to leave on her sheets and towels. His neck and shoulders seemed already capable of the broad, tenacious power of manhood. How old had Michael been when she first saw him? No older than Abe, and they had been married within the year, as soon as they could arrange it. She had wanted to wed her hands to that body forever and to the persistent youthfulness that drove it. She had been sixteen, but when she touched him, young Michael Keenan, she was permanently changed.

"How did he check you?" Miriam asked, sitting on the small stool where Abe had dropped his dirty clothes. She noticed that the shirt at her feet, the cleaner one, wasn't Abe's.

"He just pushed and poked around." Abe shifted his hips on the bottom of the tub, grimacing. "Hurt like hell at first."

Miriam reached over and turned off the water. The bathroom became quiet and manageable, a place for a mother to watch and listen. A fine heat softened the air. "And what did Tom find?" she asked, knowing how good, silent hands could work around a bruise, around all kinds of scrapes and wounds.

"Nothing but what you see," Abe said, raising his arms, his eyes only partly open in the languid steam of the bath. "He was half nice for once. Maybe we could invite him over or something. Thank him."

Miriam stood up, her arms crossed closely over her chest. Her son was drifting, almost sleeping. He breathed slowly in release. She thought that she could stand over him for a long while watching his wet ribs spread in color and stain. But she wouldn't.

"Maybe so," she said.

"And, Ma, maybe you could rub my shoulders later. After I dry off." He spoke without turning his head, as she was slipping through the door. The hair wet against his cheek was black and stark, as striking as his full lips and the size of his relaxed thighs.

"Sure," she said, backing into the cooler air of the house. "You know I will."

By the time she finished cutting the chicken, Miriam had convinced herself to have Tom Price in her house for dinner. She would do it for Abe, because she had never quite been able to silence the endless voice of her mother, the one that said a boy could never be raised without the direct molding grip of a man on his shoulder. Abe was seventeen. His father had died far away, leaving nothing but echoes that wouldn't fade. Miriam didn't see how she could have led him through childhood more honestly than she had. She'd done everything but lie to her heart and marry someone else whom her son could follow, knowing he was following shadows. She'd tried to teach and guide, do it without squeezing or scolding or hovering. And Abe had turned out all right, she thought. He knew how to take care of himself. He certainly didn't need a man to tell him how tough and swaggering he ought to be. Her son was a man, though a tentative one. She could tell by the postures of his body and the even tone of his voice. She had always given Abe what he needed, and he had, thankfully, swung right past her, out of her arms and beyond her survey. Now she would have to step back, fold into that slim pocket of motherhood where she might crouch forever. She would have to let her son go. He would have to make his own way into discovery, if there were any truth to discover.

Tom Price would be allowed into her house. She would open her doors, something she hadn't done in a long while. Then she and her son would see if they could survive the brush of strangeness. They would bear the sound and shift of a man's body in their rooms, on their floors. A body said to be handsome, firm, and empty. A body that she knew from premonition would be a well-hammered shell sealed tight around desire.

Miriam looked at the chicken limbs she had severed, the joints she had scraped and cut. Her fingers were messy and sore. She had never been much of a butcher. Then she imagined Tom Price hauling her struck-down son upstairs, touching him, bringing ease to his face. She remembered the flash of color and motion she'd seen along the paddock fence. Tom was cautious; he watched himself and others. And Miriam was sure he had an eye for her son.

They arrived late for dinner because a brood mare from Kentucky had come in behind schedule. When Miriam met Abe at the door, it was already dark. Only a few outdoor surfaces, the ones slick with continuous rain, weren't black and completely invisible. Abe came in with his boots in his hand, his fingers muddy. He kissed her, swiftly, without really looking at her, and hurried past into his room. "Sorry we're late," he said, disappearing down the hallway.

Miriam was left to meet Tom Price on her own then, and for a long moment neither one of them said a word. He just stood in front of her, half in and half out of the rain, the shoulders of his slicker shining under the porch light. His hat, an old Stetson that Abe had taken to laughing about, was in his gloved hands. He nodded at her, politely, as if he didn't know how to introduce himself. Yet he seemed to be more wary than shy. She could see it in the way he stood, tall and slightly tense, a little beyond the doorway. Miriam noted that he was all covered up; only his face and hair were free to feel the blow of the rain. She returned his nod and held the door open, pulled it wide and welcome. "Please come in," she said, affecting a small smile.

Tom Price stepped into the hall, wiping his boots on the worn throw rug that she had left beside the door. He pocketed his gloves and let his slicker, which smelled of rubber and horse sweat, drop from his shoulders. Miriam could see that he was chewing his lip as he lowered his head to push the wet hair away from his face. Abe's nervousness had rubbed off, she guessed. Her guest was on the edge of apprehension, wanting to make a good impression but not daring to go to any lengths to be false or formal. He was not good at being left alone with people, Miriam thought. Well, that was fine. She wouldn't give him any trouble. She reached out for his hat and raincoat.

"It's my fault we're behind," he said, working around his hat brim with his fingers. "Hope we haven't ruined anything."

"No, no, Mr. Price," she said, as she hung his gear on her old coatrack. "I'm glad you made it." She turned toward him, looked into a face that was dark with the shadow of a beard. "And I do mean that."

He didn't say anything else, not until Abe joined them in the kitchen, his face and hands clean, his eyes shining with an energy that Miriam was afraid she recognized. She sat the two of them at the table, served them beer, and encouraged them to talk while she finished seasoning the stew. She preferred to partic-ipate from the corner of the room, speaking as she moved from stove to counter to sink. She could turn her back, then, and her eyes wouldn't be distracted by nuance and gesture, by the mo-tions of Tom Price. Abe, of course, wanted her to sit down. Miriam guessed he wanted to actually see a circle of bodies at the table.

"Relax, Ma," he said, teasing her when she insisted on staying by the stove. "Have a beer with us first. You're like Grandma or something."

Tom laughed—he had a deep laugh—and Miriam felt herself

getting irritable. She was outnumbered, and they were going to treat her as if she were old and fussy. All right, she would sit down, she said. Just to show her son that she wasn't shy or frightened. She opened a bottle and slid into the cane-bottom chair across from Tom. His back was to the living room, and behind him, the front windowpanes were washed and distorted by the rain. She couldn't see through them. The blur of the dusk-to-dawn lights, burning weakly in the downpour, was pale and ineffectual. On clear nights she often sat at the window and watched the entire valley roll away from the sun, the land fading from a thick, continuous blue to black. Michael was the one who had watched the darkness, hour after hour. He had leaned against the haunted windows, throwing them open at the oddest times. How many mornings had she pulled him back to bed? How many suns had risen in front of him? Together they had made a child who didn't know whom to love, what to worship. And she was left to care for him—not knowing what to give, what to take, what to leave for the nights to come.

"Ma." Abe was talking to her. "Did you live at the Ridge long? With Dad? Tom's wondering if he might have seen you."

Miriam glanced at her son, then her visitor. Tom Price's eyes were yellowing, dull as an old bulb. But they were direct. She shook her head, feeling her hair rub the back of her neck. "We left for Fort Bragg long before Mr. Price arrived. He was probably in school."

"I worked my first summer in '71," Tom said. He seemed to be daring her to remember, challenging her to look back. "Pierce Walters was manager."

"No," Miriam said, shaking her head again. "Michael and I were long gone. Mr. Cabell was still alive. And Pierce was kissing his feet, he wanted to be manager so bad."

Tom showed his teeth. Like a male staking his territory,

Miriam thought. She wondered how he could be so cold and still handsome. "I've heard about Pierce," he said. "Even heard a little about your husband."

Miriam felt something stiffen—in her spine, in the air above the kitchen table. It occurred to her that Tom Price was letting her know that he was the one who ran the Ridge now. Memories were smoke, memories were worthless.

"That's the way it is with the Keenans, you know. You always hear about them, and they always *know* about you." Miriam didn't trim the edge of her voice. She pulled her fingers, quickly and cleanly, through her light-colored hair. Let him stand up for himself, she thought. Let him know there aren't any games in this household. She watched his face harden, the eyes become agate, as untrusting as an animal's. For a moment there seemed to be a palpable bitterness between them. Miriam felt it in her throat and hands, the swelling pulse to lash out. She and Tom appeared to share a sly cruelty distilled from years of having little and refusing to acknowledge the desire for more; it filled the air like a sharp warning scent. Clenching a hand in her lap, Miriam watched her clean-smelling son rise to stir the stew. He was uncomfortable, a stranger to so many scenes.

"True," Tom Price said, his hands flat and calm on the table. "It happens out here in the country. You and I've known about each other for a long time." He extended a hand toward her. "I'm pleased to finally meet you."

Miriam touched him, her fingers already tingling. His grasp was strong, unflinching. He wouldn't be compromised, not by her speculation or her probing. He wouldn't confirm anything but his presence.

"Come on, guys." Abe said, knocking a wooden spoon against the pot. "Let's eat."

Miriam laughed, but nothing was dispelled. "Your mama's getting old, Abraham. She's losing her manners."

"No kidding." He wiped his hands on his thighs. "That's why we need more people in this house."

They ate quietly in air smelling of parsley, thyme, and the juices of good beef. Abe wove most of the conversation, speaking seriously of stud fees and the spring planting of corn. He worked earnestly, without subtlety. Miriam knew he just wanted them— the man and the woman—to get along. She relaxed some and enjoyed her son's efforts, the undiminished energy of his hopes. It occurred to her, more than once, that Abe wanted her to like Tom Price, really like him. He would think of it as the finest discovery he could make, what he supposed she missed most, and the greatest gift he could give—companionship for his mother.

After supper, she followed Tom into the living room, carrying coffee; the silhouette of his body was sharp and startling. Full shoulders, a long hard back, lean hips. There was no need to guess about the pleasure that might run along such a man's skin, through his limbs and muscle. It was visible to anyone—man or woman. But that was the puzzle of Tom Price. Many were curious, but he cared for few. Watching him move to the far end of the room where the air was cool, Miriam was sure that men would be attracted to him, men who could bear the bitterness, the distance, the fleeting moment of the forbidden.

Miriam supposed that Tom Price was used to being approached, that he was often chosen and pursued. And maybe it embarrassed him, drove him a little crazy. He certainly held himself regal and high, hard on the edge of something fragile. And he kept to the farm, an isolation she understood. Sweat and cold air and the prospect of endless labor could strip and give absolution to the most troubled body. But the benediction of the land did nothing for guilt. Guilt precipitated out of even the cleanest moments and fell around everyone's feet, where it was visible and troublesome. She had come back to the valley after sixteen years in North Carolina and been able to forget nothing. She had recovered nothing but memory. And guilt.

As the three of them sat awkwardly in the living room, talk turned to the summer. Vintage Ridge was looking forward to a busy season. Mrs. Cabell was thinking of laying out a new vineyard and keeping more of the weanlings for Tom to raise and break. Tom thought, and glanced at Miriam as he said this, that he could use Abe full-time, at five dollars an hour. "He's a good worker," Tom said, clearing his throat. "And getting better."

Abe was retying his shoes, eyes on the floor. Miriam could tell they had planned this, expecting some resistance from her. Boyish, boyish games. She stared straight at Tom, leaning forward, her hands on her knees. "Can you keep him in one piece?" she asked. "That's my only concern."

"Oh, Ma," Abe said, blushing. "I won't be that stupid again."

"Maybe not. Maybe Mr. Price will be handling the stud from now on."

There was a moment of silence. Miriam hadn't realized how loudly she was speaking. "Abe and I will do our best to take care, Mrs. Keenan," Tom said, his voice modest and low.

"He's his own man," Miriam answered, seeing Abe's body sway a bit in the poor light, cutting a shape larger than she remembered. She felt old and dry around her eyes, her mouth. "It's his decision."

"Fine, then." Tom Price rose, his movement smelling crisp and a little sweet to her. "I'll take it up with Mrs. Cabell tomorrow."

Abe wanted to walk Tom to the door, perhaps to exchange

a handshake. But Miriam moved down the hallway in front of him. She had a few more things to say. So Abe waved good night and slipped into his bedroom, eager hands clasped behind his back. He could barely contain himself. Miriam smiled, biting the inside of her lip, still biting it as she turned to hand Tom Price his hat and slicker.

"Thank you," he said. "I know you don't think much of me." Miriam noticed how his fingers, broad and callused, began traveling the brim of his Stetson.

"That's not the point," she said. "My son is very fond of you. Admires you."

"No, he doesn't," he said. "He's just a kid."

Miriam swallowed. Her heart was rising through her chest, and Tom Price's hands were like wings, fluttering. She wished they weren't like wings. "Look again, Tom. He's no kid. And you know it."

"It's not the way you think, Mrs. Keenan." His voice pressed the air like a gasp or a rattle.

"It doesn't matter what I think. Abe is on his own, always has been. I, at least, want to thank you for helping him when he was hurt."

"It was nothing."

"Think what you want, but help like that is more than nothing. Don't you have family, Tom Price? Don't you know?"

"No." He glanced up, and the rise of his cheek caught the glare from the porch light. The planes of his jaw seemed sharp and unreal. "Yes," he said. "A brother, a younger one. But we're not close. We don't talk."

Miriam's anxiety blew cold with the shifting wind and rain. She felt everything fall away—his words, her body, the value of their separate, heated blood—until Tom Price was cut alone against the night on her stone doorstep. She could see he wanted her son, even from his solitude; she could see that the way a parent sees sorrow. He wanted her son, Abraham, like any animal wants a companion, a sibling, a mate. For bare comfort, for pride, for protection from the long winter blades of the future.

III

As the temperature rose and there was snow only at the crest of night, Tom began to spend his free time building a weathering for the hawk. He knew exactly what he was doing. He was sawing wood, measuring and cutting metal, anything to send him to bed with his palms pulsing and swollen. He was exhausting himself past the toss of thinking so that when he lay down to sleep, he slept a dreamless, winded sleep. He was crafting something from the fatigue of an old season. He hadn't held a bird in a long time. And whatever it was that he decided to give a name to—a kestrel, a broad-wing—it would need a place to stay. A shield from the sun and wind. A place to perch and tuck and cast when it was alone.

He would have to go north to get the bird, but that was acceptable, even a relief. He didn't usually take his vacation days because he felt that the mountains, his Ragged Mountains, were more true than the vista he could sight from any other place. Yet he had recently felt the urge to leave, an urge as cramped and pressing as any that had ever pushed against his restless body. His stomach was tight and bound. The muscles of his lower back were unforgiving. There was a limit to how much light his eyes could take before he had to quit, wipe his brow, adjust. Winter was finished and the earth was angling itself toward the sun, but it was more than that. At bottom, at the

very floor of his body, Tom knew that he would have to leave
because of Abe.

He had kept all his promises. The ones he'd made to himself,
repeated as a litany when he walked the fence-lines in the evening. The ones he'd made to Abe's mother, Miriam Keenan of
the moon-blue eyes. He and Abe had done nothing but work
together. They spoke little, ate their lunches separately, and
when Tom saw Abe waiting for him on the steps to the apartment, he drifted down the aisle of the barn, accumulating new
chores with every quiet step, increasing both his discipline and
his resignation. He allowed himself no more than the shade and
flutter of fantasy. Only the barest shiver of pleasure brushed his
mind. To have entertained less would have invited the collapse
of love; to have wanted more would have assured frustration
and longing—Tom knew himself well. He was able to watch
Abe and dwell on the bird that he would acquire to come
between them, thinking that soon all his time would be honed
by labor and care. A bird would demand much and give nothing,
nothing but the innate and frozen beauty of its wings in stoop
and glide. Abe would want to give. He was young and apt to
be generous. If anything happened, Tom told himself, they
would be fools and a danger to each other. But a hawk, a
contained bird of prey, could never fail him.

So the weathering took shape. Tom told Abe that it was
nothing, just a way for him to practice his carpentry, though he
knew Abe understood that he wasn't the kind of man who built
something without purpose. Abe could see that he was making
a shelter. There were drawings for windows pinned to the board
in his office. The foundation for three narrow walls had been
laid out behind the equipment shed. And a bundle of specially
ordered bamboo had arrived on a Saturday while Abe was there
to measure it with his curiosity. Still, Abe didn't say anything.

He didn't ask any questions, didn't whisper a single sentence. On the steps or in the office, he would always engage in conversation about something else. He would talk about foals or soil content, wood treatment or the weather. He'd mention school, or some book he'd just read, to see if Tom knew it or its landscape. But he always seemed prepared for silence, as though he couldn't be disappointed even if Tom barely answered. Abe's eyes remained as blue and steady as a broad summer twilight no matter how Tom responded.

Tom was certain he would never know what Abe really wanted. He'd understood many men in his life—some he'd known far beneath the web of flesh and bone, into the awful fire of heart. Some he knew only as weight and fear, smell and distrust—never as face, never as a body that was stable and true in daylight. And he'd known boys, a few sullen, impatient children who were the sons and brothers of someone else. But he didn't know Abe, not the way a boss or a friend or a watcher should. He understood Miriam Keenan completely. She fleshed herself out with her own tongue and the pierce of her stone-sharp eyes. They—Tom and Miriam—knew each other. Yet Abe was somehow without shape, not molded by need, still malleable within the space of his own desires. He was growing. Abraham—fruit of his mother's grief—was now the weed in a lonely man's heart.

So Tom built a home, a refuge for an animal with affectionless eyes and a cry that sounded a single note. He was moving backward, straight back in time even as spring and its promises unfolded before the rest of the world. He had always built weatherings with his brother, Quint. They had known birds together—trained and raised them, fed and molted and flown them arm by arm in fields rippling with dove and mice. They had learned together. They'd been a team. And though Quint would surely choke to deny it, as Tom choked to remember, they had fought bare and hard over a girl—Nell, a willow of a thing who tasted of cedar or berry or rock salt, and who Quint had borrowed from Tom one long afternoon. That, more than anything, had made them brothers, had opened between them a deep, hot abyss which they could neither cross nor turn from.

Abraham, however, never mentioned girls, never tongued the word woman. But Abe's mother had all the twist and flex of womanhood. A form as permanent and full as the mountains, a voice as variable and sultry as the winds. Miriam Keenan would taste like autumn and smoke, like a rare heart of hickory, Tom thought. He had been all over and through her in his mind. She stood solid and decisive, every move of her body as clutching and lovely as the sway of a tree line. And yet she didn't clasp Tom to her. And he didn't think he really wanted her. She wasn't a woman who could accept all his passions into her arms. Miriam could only be a guardian. She'd foretell his desires and missteps, and would always be too wise to warn him. It was her son—singular, young Abraham—who seemed to have limbs for the world, arms and legs and voice for anyone, even a dirty loner, to hang himself upon.

And that was how Tom would have to see himself—as a dirty, greedy man—if he kept on. Each time he braced himself against Abe's slick, bare shoulder to climb into the loft, each time he guided the boy's hands into the engine of the tractor or along the belly of a mare, he faced the thirst and perversity of his isolation. He wondered why he had released those mares into the paddock that morning, why he had felt so compelled to trap him, to see him get hurt. He had thought that he was above the seduction of fatherless children. There were men out there in the form of embrace. But since he had never taken care to cull or sift his memories, he truly could not remember whether he'd first unzipped himself in a garage, a field, or against the warm concrete wall of a restaurant kitchen. He had been in each of those places—alleys and alcoves, a shy, fearful dark-ness—but had refused to attach himself to the spilling, jerking hope they pretended to offer. Years passed. He took what he needed when his anger and the pounding, beautiful winter rain weren't enough to keep him alone. He wasn't ashamed, hadn't felt guilt or any tilt of weakness since he'd left home, backed away from the small, jealous nub of his family, erasing Quint from his heart. He hadn't even felt the need to keep women—those pale, frantic shadows of Nell—out of his life. He still took women; they became leaner, tangier, easier to understand as he aged. They loved him, they said, how they had to ride and ride, stroke him from shiver to poise to exhaustion.

Now there was Abraham, just as there had been others, fluid and round-eyed, with the muscled stride of young animals. But Abe was different, somehow nagging and featureless. His ea-gerness to farm and learn and talk wasn't childish but true. He didn't know coyness, didn't sway or pose his charms in a delib-erate manner. It had been a long time since Tom had eyed a boy without guile, a young man without mask. Abe was much the way Tom wished he might have been had he learned to cherish what he already possessed.

He and Quint were beautiful. Their silent mother had mur-mured their perfection with watery eyes, and their father, even from his stiff distance, knew beauty when he saw it. Throughout their childhood they were well cared for, cupped in a world of rich grace and intelligence until the shell of their fine skins could hardly be separated from the polish of their fine lives. Only in summers were they allowed to run free and dirty. Tom and Quint had really grown up in the fields and woods around the cottage. There, they challenged and quarreled with each other.

They met with other boys to smoke and swallow from a stolen flask. They shared the clumsy secrets of girlish bodies, Quint flushed and unruly at the sight or sound, Tom thick-tongued but fascinated. And somewhere, not far from their parents' summer home, though at a great distance of spirit, the brothers trained and flew their first bird.

It wasn't easy work. Their teacher, Mr. Ezekiel Hart, an old farm steward, was an exacting, hard-driving son of a bitch. Only men can fly birds, Mr. Hart told them time after time. Men whose respect is unyielding, whose loyalty can never be broken. I don't give a damn whether you love them or not, he'd say. Birds don't need or want love. All they need is food and a chance to beat the air.

Tom and Quint were very able. They were driven and passionate and single-minded enough to train a pair of male sparrow hawks in one season. The next summer they were bringing a buzzard, then Mr. Hart's old red-tail to fist. They couldn't get enough of those birds—the feeding, the grooming, the hours of practice with the lures. They followed the old steward in and out of the peat-scented mews, hanging on his every word, memorizing his rules and opinions as they lay back on their narrow beds at night. Together, they practiced the piercing whistle that drew hawks out of the sky. At an age when everything is expected, they had something special—a knowledge of the hunt, an elegant and respectful understanding of quick beak and talon.

Unlike all the other pursuits of boyhood, falconry found Tom and Quint evenly matched. Tom was almost a year older, but the wide, swathing personality that drew people to Quint often left Tom in the wake of his younger brother. Quint was a better athlete, a finer talker, the easier boy to know and be known by. Tom was more intelligent, but the instincts that later made him an exquisite horseman and a ranging scholar were slow to bloom.

Quint was taller, louder, stronger. Tom looked like the son of his slight, dark-haired mother, and his relatives claimed there was something to be said for that, even though they never went on to define what the advantage might be. Everyone, especially Tom's parents, tended to leave him alone.

With the birds, Tom found creatures capable of actions and glances far more disdainful than his own. Quint wanted to train the birds, to coax, bait, and lure them with the energy of a coach. Tom wanted to understand them. Each time he raised a gloved fist to remove a bird's hood, each time he fingered the handmade jesses that dangled from the tense yellow ankles, he questioned the animal's intentions. He wondered why they didn't leave forever. He wondered why they didn't rise and fly after their own game, feast and rest when they wanted. Expressionless, the birds answered on the wing. Usually, they returned to the dirty meat of the lure. Sometimes, they did not—other prey or a stray notion to fly without purpose would distract them and they'd glide out of sight, the bells of their jesses singing thinly above the breeze. Quint and Tom and Mr. Hart always retrieved them later. The birds wanted food and enjoyed habit. They soared or perched loose for a while, but they never seemed to want to be free. When asked, Mr. Hart said that hawks and falcons made no distinction. An animal cannot escape, he told Tom, when it has never been captured.

Nonetheless, Tom made a hawk leave him once, cutting the bird's bells and jesses and throwing his fist to the sky, launching the startled bird without his usual tenderness. The hawk was young, a sun-eyed female that flew beautifully, but didn't know enough to be confused when Tom didn't toss a lure or try to whistle her down. He let her go, dropping the knife-cut jesses into the damp meadow grass and stripping his thick, leather glove from a hand that was wet and shaking. Quint was somewhere with Nell, naked and unruly, smeared and oblivious in his success. Tom was more broken than jealous. He had been with Nell. She had wanted him, not Quint, very badly, she said. It was an ache, an ache right here, she said, pulling up her shirt to bare her ribs and pink-tipped breasts. And they had fallen together, she placing his hands, urging him down while she cried the music that he knew he ought to want to hear forever, even above the blank wash of release.

But it was no good. He wanted her in greed and eagerness, not in desire and certainly not for love. Before he was seventeen, Tom Price understood his limits. Women were mystery—he could spend hours watching his mother or following every trace of Nell with his senses. Men, however, were a grave secret that pretended to be open male fact. He could learn from women, survey them. Men, with their denial, their attacks and fear, always left him well below speech. Tom's rivalry with Quint delivered this permanent knowledge. His brother could have Nell because he wanted, truly wanted her. He could strip and arch without thinking or knowing that the skin, the drive, the motion were somehow false. Tom's loss of Nell, a loss coupled with relief and shot through with temporary panic, didn't kill his brother for him. The future did. Tom Price would live as he had to live. He would cut loose his hawk and leave. Quint would not and could not know his brother. It wasn't part of their fraternity. It never would be.

Tom hadn't spoken to Quint in years. His brother was married now, husband of a woman whom Tom imagined as honey-skinned and plump with the contentment of childbearing. Tom didn't imagine his brother had changed one whit, though he was a banker or broker or some damn thing. Quint would always be broad and pleasing, a heavy slab of goodwill. He would doubtless be willing to take Tom back into his life. He would be mildly proud to introduce his brother to his wife, and take wistful pleasure in showing Tom pictures of his dark-haired, hazel-eyed daughter, who looked so much like her uncle. But Tom swore that he would never give Quint the chance, never again. He had learned, all those years ago, the one thing he needed to know. Don't grieve, he had told himself, the mottled hawk circling above him in a silence that made her shape a vision. Don't grieve yourself toward pity, don't bend yourself toward pain.

So Tom spent weeks building the weathering alone. He was meticulous in his craft. Still, the blows of the hammer and the strokes of the saw weren't able to ease the buckle of desire that he felt when Abe's sweat or breath was close enough to taste. Twice in one week he went to a place, two counties over, that was thick with the smoke and perfume of men, where hands and lips would be borrowed in exchange for drinks or the burning, promising looks of anger that Tom found so easy to wear. He left relieved and without humiliation. He refused to regret the brief, biting way of men. But his relief was transient. As distinct as a whole moon, the image of Abraham rode above the vague faces and flickering tongues that spoke and swallowed without definition or true intent. Abraham continued to clear away the night. He remained potent in Tom's mornings. A silent vessel waiting to be filled, a cool vessel wanting to be fired.

IV

Abe taught himself to understand his body. Since he didn't have a father or brothers, he watched himself grow and remembered what he saw. Sometimes he tested his size and power against other boys, but he did it without much interest. His greatest pleasure came from measuring his agility by his own code. He could unload a feed truck in ten minutes. He could jump the fence surrounding his house flat-footed, without a second thought. He could stack hay, bale after bale of alfalfa or timothy, and never get sore. The horses at the Ridge, even the weanlings, were stronger and faster than he was, but he was usually able to keep them in hand. He knew he could learn from animals, especially the daring ones, so he watched the young bulls and foals and even the shy, flushed quail. His mother was easy to talk to, but he preferred his sort of understanding— a patient, hard-earned awareness of how he fit into the world.

He was sure that his watchfulness had spared him the long days of ungainliness, even ugliness, that so many of his schoolmates seemed to suffer. He'd been a little lucky too. He knew from the few pictures of his father that he'd been blessed with what his mother saucily called the Grace of the Keenan Boys. His father had been dark-eyed, black-haired, mannish in a youth that ended too soon. He'd worn a beard when his mother first met him and was tall for his age. Eighteen years old or not, Michael Keenan had promised something the other boys couldn't even sense, she said. And though she didn't take the time or the risk to name it, Abe thought he could see his promise in the photographs. Michael in a John Deere cap, no shirt, no boots, just a can of beer and a hint of what he feels for the girl who is taking the picture on his lips. Michael and Miriam outside the church, young and married, without the tense grins or the long pose of seriousness—the photo is quick and blurred, running with the smear of Miriam's falling bouquet. Another of Michael when he finished basic training, trimmed, clean-shaven, still eager. He isn't smiling above the press of his uniform, though the turn of his eyes is unmistakable—he is ready, but loving Miriam from afar, beyond the camera and heavy drape of flag that falls behind his shoulder.

Abe studied the pictures of his father, but he didn't talk to him. His father's voice was a voice he had never heard, though he imagined that his own clean baritone was bound to be similar. Instead, Abe spoke to his mother, and when she talked of his father, her eyes welled with laughter and loss. He believed every story his mother told. He believed in the gripping, loving spirit of Michael Keenan. And when he watched his mother retreat into her empty room at night or when he spread his chest with breaths of air as he stood in front of the mirror, he knew what he'd have to feel before he understood love.

Tom Price was a sort of testing ground, one way to try a few guided fingers of feeling. If Tom liked him, respected him, became someone Abe might call a friend, he reasoned that he would be able to reconstruct the life his parents had left behind. He would farm on Ivy Creek for the rest of his life. He'd buy his mother a real house, coax her to go out and rediscover the beauty of the night. Maybe he'd stay at the Ridge until Tom got old or was lured away by one of the wealthy breeders across the county. Maybe he'd start his own place.

So he busted his butt for Tom Price, and thought he'd made progress when Tom hired him for the summer, but he was frustrated and a little hurt when Tom kept his distance and started giving Elleck a few of his old chores. He did everything he could to get Tom to trust him—stayed on after hours, cleaned the barns and shed more often than usual, hung around on the apartment steps in case there was something else Tom might want him to do. He made sure that his work spoke for itself. He stayed away from Tom's personal business. He didn't know why the man was spending so much time redesigning the area behind the equipment shed, but he didn't ask. He'd tried asking Tom about the Cabells, the university, the plans for the new vineyard, but all he got was a still pair of eyes. A mouth without a smile. Looks of displeasure that he thought he should learn to accept. What he and Tom did with their hands and shoulders and straining backs was all that ought to matter. Abe remembered the clear outline of his father and how talk had never really gotten a Keenan anywhere.

He could hardly believe his anger then, the real shaking and sweating in his palms, when Tom asked him to clean the back stalls again. A valuable mare was coming down from Maryland, another one from New York, and Tom said he wanted the bedding to be perfect. Mrs. Cabell's orders. But the bedding was perfect. Abe had spent over an hour raking the shavings free of splinters and wood chips. The racks and buckets had been wiped clean, the waterers were full and working fine. Chores like these were easy for Abe. Any groom, any child could do them well.

And yet, Tom wanted it done again, even better. Abe gripped the rake handle hard, crossed the well-tended aisle, and looked over the stalls. They were exactly the way they should be, bedding up to his ankles and smelling of sweet resin. What the hell did Tom want? He'd been exacting all week but this, Abe thought, was just plain ridiculous.

He went back into the office where Tom was bent over a stack of grain receipts. "I don't understand," he said. "They look fine to me."

Tom didn't move for a moment. Then he turned—slowly, deliberately, his weight shifting onto the large hands that were flat on the desktop. He didn't say anything. His eyes were like mixed metal, smaller than Abe had ever seen them. His mouth was cold, brittle, thin as his patience. Abe felt his own anger draw into a fist below his lungs. God damn, he thought. The man has no limits.

"Check the windows," Tom said. "Look this time."

Abe left the office, pulling a clean rag from the tack trunk as he walked out. He made an effort to walk silently, to breathe without a whistle of frustration. Tom wanted to be a son of a bitch, okay. He'd polish those stalls with his shirtsleeves if he had to, get out of there, come back tomorrow as though nothing had ever happened. Tomorrow, Tom would be as steady as a wheel, busy concentrating on the scheduled breedings. Tomorrow, Tom would be all right.

Abe hung his rake on the hook outside the feed room and returned to the stalls. He examined the windows, which were high and deep-set, good for light and a small amount of fresh air. The frames and bars were solid and unbroken though the sills, not surprisingly, were dusty. Moving into the first stall and standing on his toes, Abe took a closer look. No bare nails or screw heads, no wasp nests. Nothing but dust from the shavings and the beige drapery of cobwebs.

Well, fuck Tom Price if he wants the cobwebs taken down, if he wants his mares to live in a Holiday Inn, if he wants his assistant to be busy as shit. All right, Abe thought, pulling the rag tight between his hands. All right. I'll give Tom Price exactly what he wants.

He didn't bother to drag the stepladder from the equipment shed. Instead, he pulled himself up into the shallow window well, and hooking his left arm around one of the vertical iron bars, he swung at the webs with his balled fist. The dust he stirred just made him work faster, though his eyes watered and his tongue soon tasted like chalk and the crumbled wings of insects. He figured that once he'd removed the worst, a damp cloth would wipe things clean enough for Tom. Shit, ten minutes work and he'd have the place looking better than his own home. As if the Goddamn mares would care.

He stood to reach the webs that hung like old ropes and nets along the first rafter. His nose started to run. He wished his eyes weren't burning; he could barely see. Leaning for a hand-hold near the ceiling joint, he realized, almost calmly, that his palm was slick and a little cramped. It wouldn't hold. As he began to fall, his legs tangling and his balance dropping below the point of his control, Abe cursed himself. He'd been stupid. He'd made the wrong move.

He landed on his ankle, banging and scraping his knee and jaw as he collapsed in the corner of the stall. He hadn't heard the ankle pop or anything but, God, it was already numb and his foot felt thick and useless when he tried to flex it. His cry— a bitten-off shout of surprise and anger—echoed through the barn and came to rest in the dizziness behind his eyes. Spread out on the pine-sweet bedding, his face and knee started to bleed. Abe lay as still as he could. He reached to unlace his boot. God damn, even that hurt.

Pain and embarrassment drew in his senses so close that he didn't see Tom in the doorway of the stall at first. When he did see him—standing with his feet spread apart, one hand fingering a belt loop—he pretended not to notice. Instead he tried to stand up, reaching down to dust off his jeans as he moved, shaking his head as though he might be laughing at his own foolish mistake. But he'd no sooner taken a step, staring squint-eyed and mad at Tom the whole time, than the lead-weight bones of his ankle gave way. He practically fell to his knees. As he squatted unevenly, coughing from dust, he thought he saw Tom shift a little, even flinch.

"I'm all right," he said. "Just give me some time."

Tom didn't say a word, though he didn't turn to leave or step in to help. The silence began to bother Abe. The man did nothing but look at him.

"Go on, Tom. I'll finish the Goddamn job. You know I will." Abe was surprised by his own impatience. He felt his neck throb in rhythm with his ankle. "Leave me alone, all right?"

"That ankle's not taking any weight." Abe could hardly hear him. The voice seemed to have less push than a breeze.

"It's numb is all. I landed on it." Go on, go on, Abe wanted to yell. Don't stay all over me. Not after this.

"It needs to be looked at." Again, the words were tentative, touched with what sounded like regret, sorrow heard from a distance.

"Come on." Abe scrambled to his feet, leaning against the wall for support. "Everything is fucking fine. Just let me finish the job." But he fell again when he tried to walk out the door. The joints of his foot wouldn't bend. Abe felt the corners of his eyes sting with pain and shame. He didn't have a choice. He was going to have to hop out of there, like a kid or a broken old man. He pleaded with his body to do what he wanted.

"Take that boot off." Tom stood over him, but he was bending stiffly, as if he didn't want to breathe on Abe. "You've got to get it off before the ankle swells."

"Shit."

"I'll help you."

Tom unlaced the boot quickly, though the laces seemed to become more knotted in his hands. Abe watched him hover over the foot the way he would hover over a busted girth, with craft and concentration. He inhaled through his mouth. When he was ready to work the boot free, he said that it might hurt and was sorry if it did. Then he started to pull, applying steady force at Abe's heel, wiggling the boot until it loosened. Abe, lying back on his elbows, tried to relax. All he could see was Tom's tangled hair, the dark spread of his squatting thighs, and one hand—long and light in the shadows.

The ankle was stiffening; every motion sent a whipcrack of pain to Abe's head. He talked to keep from yelling.

"You always get what you fucking want from me," he said, clenching his eyes shut as Tom pulled. "Every time."

Tom didn't respond. Maybe he slowed down some while he worked his fingers toward the top of Abe's socks, but Abe couldn't be sure. Because the silence was suddenly heavier than talk-filled air could ever be. There was real weight in their isolation, there was meaning in their pose. Abe lay back, his head pillowed on shavings, his face haloed by dust that was no longer hard to breathe. Tom removed his socks one after another, with unbroken motion, and he was so steady that it was a moment before Abe realized that there were hands exploring his bare skin.

Abe thought he understood. Tom didn't blame him or think he was clumsy. Instead he probably felt it was his fault. Abe was injured, Abe was raging, and for once, Tom Price was going to let the lashes of pain and anger fall on him. He wasn't one to say he was sorry, but he might want forgiveness. Abe sensed sadness in the hand that held his tender heel.

"Okay, Tom. Thanks." Abe thought he knew how to forgive.

And yet there was something akin to terror and great heaves of feeling on Tom's face when he raised it. His eyebrows were high, his lips were open and wide, on the edge of sound. His eyes were round, sinking into the white-gold of sunlight, drawing back as if they couldn't assimilate the color and form they saw.

"You know what you sound like," Tom said, his words almost shapeless. "You sound like a big boy."

Abe felt a tingle in his leg—maybe Tom had found a break or fray—but the tingle blushed to a roar and then a heartbeat in his ears. He read the lips above him, felt as though he heard the man's face soften in the wash of longing, a face like his mother's—handsome, naked, cracking with the weight of time. He lay flat, his head empty of the pulse that was pounding in his stomach, and he looked into the barn's rafters. Above him, birds were gliding and perching and picking their feathers clean. The sparrows cut and darted. The swallows plunged. Abe wished he could see himself with eyes so glasslike and distinct.

The hands on his arch were firm. Abe felt as if the center of his body was being stretched and stroked. He was on the verge of being swept under Tom, as though he were being rubbed with sweat and leather and the sweet glide of glycerin soap. He couldn't tell anymore if his skin was being pressed by fingers or lips.

"Your ankle's close to broken."

"Leave it alone."

"I can't."

He was drawn underneath—where a man might weep or shout or take himself apart. He felt warm with exhaustion, as if he'd run a mountain pass or forded a river in the winter cold. Everything was closing—his eyes, his ears—everything but the blood-rushed surface of his skin. Tom had him where he'd always held him. In his hand, just below the waterline of desire.

"Leave it," he murmured.

"I won't. Not anymore."

He knew, finally, what it meant to be paralyzed. He was able to move—both his hands were shaking—but his reflexes, the instinct to curl up and hide, had left him. Tom's hand was right above his knee, resting, not gripping. And that hand was all he recognized. He couldn't recall the details of his life, the shape of his face, the sound of his own voice in his head. He tried to make his name come together—Abraham, Abe—but he couldn't. The sounds were quiet and soft and made no sense.

It wasn't fear that he swallowed when the hand reached for his belt, or if it was fear, then it was hotter and more liquid than he expected. He waited for his legs to draw up and run, but they didn't. Tom talked to him, or maybe he was coaxing himself, saying one word—*easy, easy, easy*—as though he was comforting a halter-broke colt. Abe's head filled with sweet air. Two hands and a gentle voice. It could have been a lullaby. It could have been.

The silent zipper, the cool dry reach, a long flat face turned away. Abe squeezed his elbows against his sides, jolted, thinking damn you, damn you, God damn, but he couldn't think of any more words and he couldn't make a sound out loud. The hand was there, there and always there, fingerless but not frightened. It was easy. Easy. The blood under his skin felt like a fluttering sheet, then a wide ribbon. He closed his eyes and tried not to gulp for the air he needed. He knew his legs were pinned under Tom's, he knew that, but he thought if he didn't move and never made a sound, that time would pass or stop or slow down and nothing would happen the way it seemed to be happening now.

He wanted it to be another body that shivered when it heard the groan, the smooth, human sound that rose for one second above the hands. He wanted it to be another body, another blood-filled skin that felt the shape of the mouth, hotter and wetter than fear. He thought that if Abe had really been there he would have screamed or swung his fists. Easy. Easy.

The wrestle of shapes behind his eyes burned to a thin white line of ash. The damp noise, the heavy crouch weren't real, they weren't. His body was burning and arcing, punching and boiling away from him. He was inside Tom, punching.

And Tom recoiled as if there were no resistance; he wasn't even there, hovering, absorbing everything there was.

He never wanted to see Tom's face again, and he knew he never would, not naked or gentle or greedy. Instead, the face would come to Abe behind his squeezed and aching eyes, a mask that would be his memory. It hung there now, hard and frozen, and he was frightened. He knew then that fear was not what you saw in front of you but what you expected next. Thin, sun-weathered skin, the eyes hollow and wet. A man was gasping for breath, and then both men were gasping. They were the same, the two of them, for one cold blossoming moment. It was what Abe had always wanted, they were equal and the same. Abe thought he could hear it in his ears, the sort of crying men did without words or tears, breaking into the hard, separate pieces they'd have to live with. His skin was tight across his cheeks, his mouth was dry. His legs and chest were aching. He had finally lived long enough to fly apart.

V

Miriam is in the dark well of a dream.

Translucent blue walls the unchanging shade of midnight rise around her. There are no windows, no curtains, nothing to swim or wave in the cool, edgeless space. There is nowhere to go beyond the warm pool of her body. She is not frantic or afraid, though music seems to be spilling from a source high above her and the melody is not familiar. She is comforted. She is with Michael.

He is behind her. She can't see him, but she recognizes his precise grasp, the particular way he likes to take her when he doesn't feel gentle or kind. He is behind her, and he must have asked her to rise to her knees though she can't remember anything but the heavy draw of his breath, the suck that always precedes the shove of his body, followed by the solid, pinching cup of his hands on her buttocks, the leverage he uses to lift and spread her quickly. He doesn't speak, but she knows him in this scentless, sightless, pressing world. He wants her before she is ready, while she is dry and anxious for the lingering pass of fingertips, while she is still separate. So he forces himself deep and fast, never speaking, driven even harder by her sounds that are half-swallowed cries of pain. Michael hurts her as he has hurt her before, but she doesn't blame him. Even while her flesh is rubbed wide and raw, she feels his force and demand and pleasure, and she knows how quickly these will heat and melt into what will come to her as love.

Miriam's face is pressed into a white pillow she has not seen until now. She smells her own wet breath, the only scent in all this motion. Above and behind and through her, Michael is gasping, making sounds that are beyond language and contact. Miriam feels her body furrowed and ridden flat until Michael reaches around her bare thigh and locks her hips into his. There is nowhere to go. Michael is with her, within. She can almost taste his thick salt in the draped air of the room, and she smiles, her tongue dry. This time it will be a black-eyed daughter. A child with oval eyes, an oval voice, an elliptical song for the future, a keening without grief. Behind the lids of her thrumming eyes Miriam can see the ivory cradle of her pelvis, the thick, pink blanket of her womb. This time, Michael will leave her with more than he's taken.

The new child will tread their anger, pace their inability to live together as an immutable pair. Michael won't take himself away, not again. They will remain a couple, family, a charge without lessening.

He falls away. No caress, no gesture. The body heaves behind her, sprawled on a bed that now seems as long and packed as a white road. Miriam lowers herself onto her belly. Her back is stiff and damp, and she thinks she will pull Michael onto her when he awakens and comes to her again, as he always does. He will be tender. He will want to feather the body that she is sure is rocking with child. He will want to draw fingers along her throat and feel the current of his lass, his haven, the only possession he says he never shares.

Miriam shivers.

When the man behind her shifts, seems almost to pinwheel on the strand of the bed, she is at his side before his eyes are open. She will have her turn. She presses hard, wanting to fill his mouth, his ears, the sockets of his eyes. She is raking, clawing hair and sweat from his brow before she realizes that the body is hot but indistinguishable, that the face has no sheen. Straddling him, she runs her hands along a pale jaw and beaked nose she is no longer sure of. As the air around her wheels with light, she watches a pair of lids flutter. They blink marvelously as if they were just unhooded. Eyes yellow as age, yellow as yolk, yellow as crust. The mouth below opens to a glistening throat, and Miriam arches away, falls away, almost fleeing. She reaches outward as her hands lose weight, wondering where he is, the body that is not this body. Where is the one she desires?

But he cannot be found. The sound of falling planks filled her ears as she opened her eyes to find her bed flat and empty except for the uncomfortable twist of her body. A window was open. The breeze was sweet and dusty with pollen. Somewhere a door was swinging noisily in the wind, and its insistent pounding had broken her sleep.

Miriam lay still for a moment, allowing Michael and his flesh, memorized forever in youth, to drop through her heart and spine into the hard mattress. He faded as he always did, lingering only as a vague spasm in her throat, a grip that had substance but little meaning, so little depth. Her dreams were a mockery of sleep, another shade of haunting. Tom wasn't a part of her;

yet he appeared yellow-eyed in her dream. They shared nothing but a furious wish for exemption. She knew that was true. As the door banged again, erratic in rhythm, Miriam pushed her hair from her forehead and straightened her clutched arms. The house was open. Abraham must be home.

It wasn't like him to be hasty and leave the latch undone. He was tidy, not given to impulse. Miriam stood and let her skirt fall from its rumple. Barefoot, she walked into the hallway, her vertebrae somehow cramped, her eyes weak from sleep.

Abe was in the kitchen. He was sitting at the table, with his denim jacket on, his body stiff in the wind that was drawing and pulling through the house. He sat upright, his hands lying before him on the dull, creamy surface of the table. He wasn't right. Miriam could see immediately that he was off balance, about to fall away from the table lamp and the impossible foreign stretch of his hands. His face was drawn and tired, she thought, smeared with the sweat and dirt of the farm. His eyes were lidded, indistinct from a distance. Fever, she thought, approaching him, her feet more patient than her mind. But when he looked at her—and he didn't spare her the narrow blade of his eyes—he wasn't asking for the swift comfort from sickness she often provided. In fact, he didn't seem to be asking for anything at all.

"Abe, are you all right?"

He turned from her, dropping his chin to his shoulder as if he might hide beneath the flesh of his own breast, though he made no real attempt to move away. He seemed to think it was enough to be buried in his skin.

"Are you hurt?" Miriam noticed that one foot was bare, its surface mottled with dirt or bruises, she couldn't tell which. "Something wrong at the farm?"

He shook his head, swung it as though it were on its own

pendulum. It was then that she noticed the raw scrape along the incline of his jaw. He looked as if he'd been peeled, the threads of his skin frayed and torn loose. Miriam's palms burned, she wanted to touch him so much. Yet his silence was fathomless and somehow terrible. She didn't want to push him too soon. She thought if he would look at her one more time, she'd know. Know where he had been broken, see where he was parting.

"Abe, honey," she said, leaning over the edge of the table. "I'm right here."

He gave her one second of truth before his fingers curled and struck the table. One empty, running glance—the white, slack shape of the mouth, the tiny, hard safety of the eyes—told Miriam what she needed to know. Anger beat into her sudden pulse like the hammer of her son's clenched fists.

"Ma, I didn't do anything."

She placed one palm on her son's quavering head.

"Ma, I didn't help."

She thought she'd never seen bones or sweat or hair so much like glass.

Miriam's blood sang high, and she would never be sure how she was able to leave the house in all her deafness. She stopped only to pull her boots over the bare soles of her feet, leaving Abe behind in the clamor of the house. She didn't think of gathering him and holding him until the afternoon's violation was memory. She wasn't sure she could close her arms around him the right way. Even if she could, she knew that they might wrap shut on nothing. Instead, her eyes filled, and the field of their vision narrowed as she ran into the yard, skirt clasped in her stiff fingers. She no longer saw Abe or their home or the hip of the mountain ridge that was arching toward the sun. She saw a road before her, a steep path of dust and gravel. She had given the blessing of silence; she had waited. But her trust hadn't held, and now, in the halo of her ribs, she felt the tear of broken bonds like the tear of her own breastbone. Tom Price had gone too far.

She leaned downhill and drove her loosely shod feet forward, falling into the dive of her fury like a blackbird. Down the drive, north along the creek, hard uphill toward the gates of Vintage Ridge. Her wrists pounded with blood and her feet went numb. Her gasps of air were salty and sharp. As she ran, she felt her clothes shift and drop loose around her shoulders and waist. It was as if she were breaking free of everything but the flailing rod of betrayal.

Later she wouldn't remember the slight evening rush of the creek or the warm perfume of pollen and blossom. She wouldn't remember the time it took her to get to the Ridge—it seemed like seconds—or the fall that cut her hands and spilled the blood that covered everything she touched. She wouldn't recall dragging a heavy stick from a ditch. Instead she would remember feeling so sure, so pure and direct, that when the land flew past her and the trees and brush were blurred with motion, she couldn't tell the difference between branch or wing or shadow. Which was the way it should be: indistinguishable lattice, dark web without name.

She found Tom outside the barn. He was standing alone between the paddock and the shed, with nothing at his back. It was as if he were waiting for her, waiting for the gyre of pursuit. But as she drew close, her run slowed to a cautious walk, Miriam could see that he wasn't waiting, that he wasn't even aware of her. His face was turned to the sky, his chin held up toward the plunging sun. His jeans were dusty, but his shirt was tucked and buttoned, and he looked not so much like a seducer but a boy, a child who has forgotten every responsibility save his loneliness. Miriam began to shake with fatigue, wondering if she was wrong, wondering if Abraham was more like Michael—more seizing and secret—than she wanted to imagine. And she felt herself drop into the sorrow of Tom's solitude, back into the bellied hole she knew so well, until Tom lowered his chin and shifted his weight, and she saw, for the first time, the brittle, heat-baked flint of his eyes.

"What have you done, you son of a bitch. You tell me now. Now."

"Nothing he didn't want," he said. "I finished the job."

"That's not your right," she said, pulling at her loose and crazy hair. "It's nobody's right."

"It happens how it happens," Tom said, his words raspy and harsh. "I can't be sorry, because he'll get over it and learn his own mind. For once. Did you ever ask him what he wanted? Did he ever tell you one thing?"

"He's my child," she said. "I know him. You don't."

"Like you said, Miriam Keenan, he's no child. We had a deal."

"I asked you to take care of him." Miriam tried to throw her words toward him, but she felt the pulse in her neck slip to a lower beat as though something were leaving her, flowing hard and fast somewhere else.

"You're just afraid that you've failed him. You're afraid to feel at fault." Tom stared at her from under his hat brim, his face halved by shadow. "Well, it is your fault, you raised him solo and free. And now he'll live no better than the two of us. He'll get broken again. And again. Harder and worse. I'm sorry to say that to a mother, but it's true."

The sound she made next formed no word, and she swooped without caution, her arms wide with effort, her hands flecked with blood. She struck him breast to breast. Their embrace was ungiving. From above, where winds lifted dust and smoke out of the valley, the man might be shielding his face from the battery of exhausted fist or stick. Or he might be covering his lips to pierce a whistle toward the sky. Beyond gliding wingtip, where the light began to slide beneath the dark hem of the Ragged Mountains, the woman might be beating at shoulders or eyes, might be laying her stained hands on a body that held her tight, that understood her grief. And her cry—how good was the ear on a single, distant note—might be one of fury or it might be one of love.